VALENTIN

BAYOU BROTHERHOOD PROTECTORS
BOOK SIX

ELLE JAMES

TWISTED PAGE INC

ISBN EBOOK: 978-1-62695-526-4

ISBN PRINT: 978-1-62695-527-1

ISBN HARDCOVER: 978-1-62695-605-6

Dedicated to my sister. She's a badass.
Elle James

VALENTIN

BAYOU BROTHERHOOD PROTECTORS
BOOK # 6

New York Times & *USA Today*
Bestselling Author

ELLE JAMES

CHAPTER 1

OUIDA MAE MAUDET gave her classroom of fifteen-year-olds a challenging stare. "You know that if you finish your homework before you leave for the day, you won't have to do it at home—and you'll have the benefit of my help."

Ginger groaned. "Oh, Miz Mo, no one wants to stay at school any longer than they have to. And it's Friday. We just want to go."

Miz Mo, as her students referred to her, held up her hands. "Just saying. Some of you could use the assistance to improve your grade in this class. And with the test on Tuesday..."

"I got football practice," Brady Johnson said. "Coach makes us do more pushups if we're late."

The students had already started shoving their books and papers into their backpacks, ready for the bell signaling the end of the school day.

Ouida Mae's lips twisted. She couldn't blame them. She remembered being that age. All her classmates had been halfway out of their seats before every bell had rung. Only she had been the nerdy kid who had stayed after class to learn even more about biology and other sciences. Having grown up in Bayou Mambaloa, she had been surrounded by opportunities to explore and discover all the things nature had provided.

The bell rang.

Students lunged for the door, slinging backpacks over their shoulders and pulling cell phones out of their pockets.

Ouida Mae adjusted the papers on her desk and reached for her purse in the bottom drawer.

The sound of someone clearing a throat brought her attention back to the classroom she thought had been emptied.

Sophie Saulnier was still at her desk with her textbook open. She gave Ouida Mae a weak smile.

"Ah, Sophie, I didn't realize you were still here." Ouida Mae crossed her hands on her desk. "Did you need additional assistance with your homework?"

The girl swallowed hard and nodded, her cheeks flushing a ruddy red.

Ouida Mae gave her an encouraging smile. "There's no need to be embarrassed to ask for help. Where are you having the most difficulty?"

"Um, I don't know where to start." Sophie's gaze shifted toward the apple on Ouida Mae's desk.

The hungry look in the teen's eyes made Ouida Mae study her more closely. The girl was painfully thin and had dark shadows beneath her eyes. Her dark hair hung long and straight down her back. Ouida Mae would consider the girl's hair and dark eyes her best features. But she really needed to put some meat on her bones.

Ouida Mae leaned forward. "You know it's hard to study and learn when your body doesn't have the fuel it needs." Her hand curled around the apple. "When was the last time you ate?"

Sophie shrugged.

Ouida Mae's eyes narrowed. She couldn't remember seeing Sophie sitting at a table in the school's cafeteria at lunch. "Sophie, are you hungry?"

As Sophie shook her head, her stomach rumbled loudly.

"Have you had anything to eat today?" Ouida Mae asked.

Again, Sophie shrugged.

Ouida Mae stood and walked down the aisle between the desks to where Sophie sat at the rear of the classroom. "Here, you can have my apple." She handed the apple to Sophie. "As a matter of fact, I didn't eat all of my lunch today. It's still in the refrigerator in the teacher's lounge. Stay here. I'll be right back."

Though Sophie took the apple, she shook her head. "Please, that's not necessary."

"If I'm going to help you with your homework, you need to be sufficiently fueled to absorb the material." Ouida Mae lifted her chin. "I'll be right back. Stay here."

As Ouida Mae left the room, she glanced back over her shoulder, happy to see Sophie take a bite of the apple. Ouida Mae wondered when her last meal had been. She made a mental note to check with Sophie's mother to find out what was going on. In the meantime, the chicken breast and salad she hadn't eaten for lunch would make a decent meal for the teen.

While she was in a teacher's lounge, she purchased a bottle of apple juice from the vending machine, pulled the glass storage container with the chicken inside from the refrigerator, and popped it in the microwave for a minute and a half. She took the container with the salad out of the refrigerator and poured some dressing over the leafy greens from the bottle she kept stored in the refrigerator.

When the microwave beeped, she gathered the salad, the chicken and then a juice bottle and left the teacher's lounge.

The sound of shattering glass and moving furniture echoed down the hallway.

"What the hell?" Ouida Mae hurried to her classroom, which was near the end of the hall where the noise emanated. Before she reached the classroom, a door to her left opened, and a hand reached out, snagged her arm and yanked her into Miss Donna Durand's classroom.

Heart thumping, Ouida Mae juggled the containers in a desperate attempt to keep from dropping them.

Sophie stood beside her, her eyes wide and a finger pressed to her lips. "Shh," she said softly.

"What's wrong? What's happening?" Ouida Mae whispered as she set the food containers on a nearby desktop.

"A brick crashed through the window and landed on the floor by my feet," Sophie said in a voice barely above the whisper. "I dropped to the floor and crawled out of the room. When I looked back, a man dressed in black scraped the glass out of the window frame and crawled through it into the classroom." The girl wrapped her arms around her middle. "I ran. I didn't know what else to do. Then I thought about you. I couldn't let you walk into that room. I didn't know why he broke in or what he planned to do, but I couldn't let him hurt you."

Her heart warmed by the student's concern for her safety, Ouida Mae crossed to the phone hanging on the wall. A relic of the past, the phone was only used to communicate with office personnel. She lifted the receiver, hoping someone in the office was still there.

No one answered. The staff must have gone home for the evening. She returned the receiver to its cradle, pursing her lips. "My cell phone is in my purse in the classroom." She frowned. "I don't suppose you have one?"

Sophie shook her head.

The muffled sound of crashing furniture continued down the hallway.

"What do we do?" Sophie asked.

Ouida Mae debated sneaking out of the classroom and down the hallway to the office, where she could place a 911 call on the landline. That would mean leaving Sophie by herself.

That wasn't going to happen.

What if the man destroying her classroom decided to continue his destruction spree and found the girl alone and unprotected?

Ouida Mae twisted the deadbolt lock on the classroom door and glanced toward the windows. Afternoon sunlight peeked through the fluttering leaves of an oak tree in the schoolyard.

"What if he comes through the window?" Sophie asked as if reading her thoughts.

"We stay out of sight and hope he doesn't. If he does try to come through the window, it will take him time. Time enough for us to leave the classroom and get out of the school."

"Couldn't we sneak out a window?" Sophie suggested.

Ouida Mae shook her head. "Not the way the windows open." She nodded toward a desk in the back of the room. "Help me move this desk to the corner."

Student desks were built to withstand teenagers over the years of use and abuse. They were a little heavy but not so much so that Ouida Mae couldn't scoot one to where she wanted it to be. But that would make noise, and she couldn't risk making noise and drawing attention to the classroom where she and Sophie were hiding.

Between the two of them, they lifted the desk, carried it to the far corner and set it down gently without making a sound. Once it was in place, Ouida Mae tipped her chin toward it. "I need you to hide behind the desk."

Sophie dropped to her knees and scooted behind the desk. She glanced up at Ouida Mae with a frown. "What about you?"

Ouida Mae had already turned to search the room for something she could use as a weapon. "I'll be all right." The only item she could find of use was a single chair standing beside Miss Durand's desk. To reach it, she would have to pass in front of the classroom door with its narrow window. Ouida Mae stood still for a moment, listening to the sounds coming from down the hall in her classroom.

According to the amount of noise generated, the perpetrator was destroying everything he could get his hands on.

Not knowing for sure if the man was operating alone or with a partner, Ouida Mae couldn't risk being seen through that window. She dropped onto her hands and knees, glad she had on pants instead of her usual sundress. She quickly crawled beneath the window and all the way over to the desk. She placed the chair over her back and returned the same way, crawling across the floor until she reached Sophie.

The girl helped her take the chair off her back and place it gently on the floor.

Ouida Mae sat on the floor behind the chair with Sophie behind her. It was all she could do to stay put when every fiber of her being wanted to storm out in the hallway and chase the bastard out of her classroom. If she had been alone, she might have done just that, but she had Sophie to think about.

Moments later, she heard a shout in the hallway.

"What the full darn heck is going on here?"

"Jonesy," Ouida Mae and Sophie whispered at the same time.

Ouida Mae was on her feet in seconds.

"Stay here," she commanded as she grabbed the chair by its back and unlocked the door. She stepped out into the hallway in time to see Jonesy enter her classroom.

"Don't—" she started to warn the school's eldest employee.

"What do you think you're doing?" The old man demanded.

She raced down the hall with the chair held out in front of her. Ouida Mae hadn't reached her classroom before another crash and a loud thump reverberated in the building.

"Leave Jonesy alone!" she shouted as she rounded the door frame and rushed into the classroom.

A man dressed all in black, including a black ski mask, had one leg over the windowsill, ducking low to squeeze through the opening.

The anger and adrenaline coursing through her veins pushed Ouida Mae forward with her chair held high, her sights set on the escaping offender. She took two steps forward and fell over an obstruction on the floor. The chair flew from her hands, skated across the tile and came to a stop at the base of the now-empty window.

A groan brought her attention back to the obstacle that had brought her to her knees.

Mr. Jones, the school's janitor, lay on his side, a gash across his temple oozing blood.

Pushing aside the desire to discover the identity of the man who had attacked her classroom, Ouida Mae focused on the janitor. "Mr. Jones, are you okay?"

The old man groaned in response.

"Sophie," Ouida Mae cried. "Sophie!" she called louder this time. Footsteps rang out in the hallway.

The teenager appeared in the door frame. "Oh my God. Is he dead?"

Ouida Mae shook her head. "No. But I need you to get my cell phone out of the top drawer of my desk and dial 911."

The girl stood frozen, her eyes filling with tears.

With the old man lying on his side, semi-conscious, they didn't have time for tears. "Go!" Ouida Mae said.

Sophie turned and ran across the room to Ouida Mae's desk.

Ouida Mae prayed the man who had attacked Jonesy hadn't re-entered the school. If he had, they might only have seconds to place a call for help.

The old man lay still, no longer groaning.

Feeling for a pulse, Ouida Mae touched her fingers to the base of the old man's throat. For a long moment, she felt nothing. Her heart skipped several beats. Then, the slow, steady thump bumped into her fingertips. Ouida Mae released the breath she held.

He was still alive.

For now.

Footsteps pounded toward her from the direction of the office.

Sophie appeared at Ouida Mae's side, the cell phone pressed to her ear. "I dialed 911," she told

Ouida Mae and then listened, her attention on the dispatcher.

"Yes, ma'am, there's been an attack at the junior high. We need an ambulance. Jonesy—Mr. Jones—the janitor, is hurt. He's unconscious. Is he breathing?" Sophie looked to Ouida Mae,

Ouida Mae nodded.

"Yes, he's breathing, and he has a pulse." She listened. "He was dressed all in black and got in and out through a window in Miz Mo's classroom... Are we safe?" Sophie gave a nervous laugh. "I hope so. Please hurry." Again, she listened and nodded. To Ouida Mae, she said, "They're sending the sheriff and an ambulance. They want me to stay on the line."

A siren wailed in the distance, its volume increasing as it moved closer.

Afraid to leave Mr. Jones's side, Ouida Mae tipped her head toward her desk. "There's a first-aid kit in my desk. Get it, please."

Before she finished speaking, Sophie flew across the room, still holding the phone to her ear. She opened drawers, rummaged and slammed them shut one by one.

"Bottom right drawer," Ouida Mae called out.

A moment later, Sophie handed her the kit and then stood back, tears sliding down her cheeks. "Is he going to be all right?"

Ouida Mae nodded, hoping she was right. She

extracted a packet of gauze, tore it open, and pressed it to the wound on Mr. Jones's temple.

Sophie clamped a hand over her mouth. Her face blanched. She turned, grabbed a wastepaper basket and threw up what little bit of apple she'd eaten. "I'm sorry," she said into the cell phone. "No, I'm all right."

"Oh, Sophie, sweetie," Ouida Mae said. "Mr. Jones is going to be all right, and so are you." She wished she could go to the girl and hold her in her arms to reassure her. But the Jonesy needed her more.

The sirens screamed to a halt.

"Sophie, you need to go open the door at the end of the hallway to let the sheriff inside."

The girl straightened, wiped her mouth on her sleeve, and squared her shoulders. She drew in a deep breath and stepped out of the classroom, then raced down the hallway.

Within seconds, Ouida Mae's classroom was filled with first responders.

Sheriff's Deputy Shelby Taylor was the first to arrive, easing her belly out from behind the wheel. She wore a sheriff's department maternity uniform that only emphasized her very pregnant state. At over eight and a half months along, she'd cut her hours in half but insisted on working up to her due date.

"Sweet Jesus, Ouida Mae," she said, her gaze scanning the room, "what happened?"

Relief filled Ouida Mae's chest at the sight of her

friend. Tears held in her eyes, but she couldn't let them fall. Not yet. Not in front of Sophie. She blinked them back and lifted her chin. "Someone came into my classroom and destroyed it. Mr. Jones tried to stop him. Apparently, the assailant hit him."

Deputy Taylor carefully knelt beside Mr. Jones and felt for a pulse. After a long moment, she nodded.

"I was afraid to move him in case he'd suffered any spinal injuries in the fall," Ouida Mae said.

Shelby patted her arm. "You did the right thing."

Paramedics arrived, carrying a stretcher and a box filled with medical devices.

Ouida Mae stood and offered a hand to Shelby. The two women moved out of the way to allow the emergency medical technicians to do their job.

Ouida Mae retrieved her purse from her desk and cell phone from her student. "You did good, Sophie."

The teen stared around at the mess.

Finally able to assess all the damage, air lodged in Ouida Mae's lungs. Every desk had been toppled or flung across the room. Her own desk had been slammed against the wall sideways. But the red paint on the walls was like open, bleeding wounds, with messages that frankly frightened Ouida Mae.

MIZ MO THE HO
DIE BITCH!
SAY NO TO SEX ED
EVOLUTION IS BLASPHEMY

LEAVE OR DIE!

"Why would someone do this?" Sophie asked, her voice quiet as if she stood in a library.

Ouida Mae touched the girl's arm. "I don't know."

As the medics stabilized Mr. Jones and eased him onto the stretcher, Ouida Mae slipped an arm around Sophie's shoulders and pulled her against her.

The student's body trembled uncontrollably.

"Oh, sweetie," Ouida Mae rubbed the girl's arm. "He's going to be OK. They're going to take care of him."

"I'm glad Mr. Jones will be okay," Sophie said. "That could've been us," she added in a whisper, her body shaking so hard her teeth rattled.

Ouida Mae pulled Sophie into her arms and hugged her close. Even though the student was taller than the teacher, it didn't matter. To Ouida Mae, Sophie was a child and needed comfort.

Shelby, Ouida Mae and Sophie followed the paramedics as they carried Mr. Jones out of the school and loaded him into the ambulance. Once they had him situated, one of the paramedics turned to Sophie and Ouida Mae. "Are you two okay?" he asked.

Ouida Mae nodded. "I am, but please check my student, Sophie. She might be in shock."

"Have her parents been notified of the incident?" the paramedic asked.

"I'm okay," Sophie said quickly. "I'd better get home before anyone worries about me."

Ouida Mae shook her head. "Not by yourself."

"Seriously, I'm fine," Sophie insisted as she backed out of Ouida Mae's arms. The girl turned and hurried away.

Ouida Mae turned to Shelby. "Do you need me for anything else?"

Deputy Taylor shook her head. "If I have questions, I'll give you a call or have you come by the station." Her friend followed Ouida Mae's gaze. "Do you want me to follow her?"

Ouida Mae's eyes narrowed. "No, I'll do that. I don't think she has a good home situation and is embarrassed by it. I'll follow at a distance, just to make sure she gets there all right."

"Are you sure?" Her friend frowned. "The perpetrator only trashed *your* classroom. Based on what he spray-painted on the walls, you were the target. You might not be safe."

"I'll keep my eyes open. I just can't let that child go home alone." Ouida Mae left her friend standing among the first responders and hurried after Sophie.

She thought she'd lost her until she spotted the girl ducking between two houses. Glancing over her shoulder often, she followed the girl through the streets of Bayou Mambaloa to what appeared to be a deserted shack perched on the edge of the water on stilts. She climbed into a pirogue, lifted a paddle and pushed away from the shore. As she back-paddled into deeper water, she glanced up, and her gaze met Ouida Mae's. She mouthed the words, *I'm okay*.

With no way to follow her student, Ouida Mae walked to the shoreline and called out, "I'm here if you need me, day or night. I mean that."

"Thank you," Sophie said.

"No. Thank *you*. You saved me," Ouida Mae said. She watched the teenager paddle away into the bayou, wishing she could follow her all the way home. She wanted to make sure the girl had the support she needed at home after experiencing such a traumatic incident.

Ouida Mae suspected she did not have that support. She wondered if she had anyone to help her. As thin and hungry as she'd appeared, she could use a friend and someone to check on her situation at home.

Ouida Mae pulled out her cell phone and called Shelby.

"Is everything all right?" the sheriff's deputy answered on the first ring.

"I don't know." Ouida Mae described how Sophie had paddled away into the bayou. "I'm worried about her."

"Frankly, I'm worried about both of you." Shelby sighed. "I'll take the sheriff's boat out in a little while and check Sophie's home situation. We're too short-handed to station a deputy at the school, but I might have an alternative."

"Good." Ouida Mae's hand tightened on the cell phone.

"I hate to think of what might have happened if all the students had been in the classroom when the man attacked," Shelby said.

Ouida Mae nodded, even though Shelby couldn't see her. "Me, too."

CHAPTER 2

VALENTIN PUSHED through the heavy doors at the front entrance of the Bayou Mambo Junior High at eight o'clock Saturday morning.

He'd received a voicemail from his team lead, Remy Montagne, in the middle of the night, asking him to be there.

"I'll explain then," Remy had added to the end of the message.

Valentin had been out in the bayou frog gigging with Mitchell Marceau, the local marina owner, when the message had come through. Given the late hour, or early in this case, Valentin had refrained from calling Remy for clarification.

They'd already collected all the frogs Mitch needed to supply the Crawdad Hole Bar and Grill and had been heading back to the marina when Valentin had gotten the message.

Curious and still wired from the hunt, Valentin had returned to the boarding house where he'd been staying since coming on board with the Bayou Brotherhood Protectors.

What could be happening at the local junior high on a Saturday morning that required the protectors to be in attendance?

Valentin had stripped down to his boxer briefs and lay across the comforter with his hands laced behind his head, staring up at the ceiling, imagining different scenarios.

Maybe Remy wanted the Brotherhood Protectors to help out at a school function. Valentin had planned on sleeping in that morning, but he shrugged that thought off. Whatever Remy had in mind would probably only take half a day or less, and Valentin would have the rest of the day to himself.

When he arrived in the junior high parking lot, he was surprised to find only a few vehicles there and no children. Among the vehicles were Remy's truck and a Parrish Sheriff's SUV. That fact didn't concern him too much, as Remy's wife was Deputy Shelby Taylor. He didn't recognize the other vehicles.

No one waited at the reception desk for his arrival or to guide him to wherever he was to meet his team lead. Voices sounded from behind the counter and down a short hall. He followed the sound to an open doorway and stepped into a conference room with five people seated at the end of a long table, four of which he recognized. Remy occupied one of the seats with Shelby at his side. Across the table from them was Sheriff Bergeron and Landry Laurent, another member of the Brotherhood.

"Oh good, you're here." Remy waved a hand toward an empty seat and turned to the older woman wearing a black blazer and cream blouse seated at the head of the table. "Principal Ashcraft, this is Valentin Vashon, one of the Bayou Brotherhood Protectors on my team and the man I had in mind for this mission." Remy turned to Valentin. "Valentin, this is Ms. Ashcraft, the principal of the Bayou Mambaloa Junior High."

Valentin crossed the room and extended his hand to the principal. "Nice to meet you, ma'am."

The woman's eyes narrowed as she reluctantly accepted his hand and greeting. "Mr. Vashon, the pleasure is mine." She dropped his hand and turned to Remy. "I don't know," she said. "He's not exactly what I would've pictured to play the part," she said. "Do you have anyone who is less..." she struggled as if searching for an appropriate word, "less intimidating?"

Remy chuckled. "The men on our team are all combat veterans who spent a number of years on active duty fighting for our country. Excuse them if they tend to look a little intimidating. But trust me, they can get the job done. Valentin and Landry are no exception."

Valentin dropped into an empty chair, a frown pulling at his brow. "What's going on? Did you call us in to take on a mission?"

"Yes," Remy said.

"No," Principal Ashcraft spoke simultaneously.

Remy pressed on. "I take it you haven't heard that the school was attacked last night. A man broke into a classroom, trashed it and spray-painted the walls with threats. He seemed to be focused on the one classroom assigned to the science teacher. Shelby answered the call last evening and brought it to my attention."

"Was anybody injured?" Valentin asked.

"Yes," the principal responded. "Our janitor, Mr. Jones."

Deputy Taylor added, "He was knocked unconscious. He hasn't regained consciousness yet."

"One of the students and our science teacher were in the building at the time, hiding in another classroom until Mr. Jones was attacked," Principal Ashcraft said. "Miss Maudet ran after Mr. Jones to warn him but was too late. The attacker escaped after hitting the janitor."

"Miss Maudet is a friend of mine," Deputy Taylor said. "She and the student were pretty shaken by the experience."

VALENTIN

Remy picked up from there. "Our team can help in this situation. They are sworn protectors."

"I'm not so sure your team *can* help," Principal Ashcraft said. "The children are my primary concern. Your men haven't been cleared through the state's strict background check."

"Principal Ashcraft," Remy said, "My men have been through some of the most stringent background checks, securing federal top-secret clearances. They've been entrusted with information critical to the security of our nation and our people. I trust them with my life, your life, and the lives of each and every one of the children under your care."

The principal's lips press together in a tight line. "There has to be another way."

Sheriff Bergeron leaned his arms on the table and fixed his gaze on Principal Ashcraft. "I don't have the staff to assign an officer to the school. Your PE teacher, Miss Sutton, informed you she was not coming back until the assailant has been identified and incarcerated."

Deputy Taylor added, "You're short a PE teacher and a janitor. Your students and staff are at risk and will likely be scared. The other alternative is to shut down the school until the perpetrator is caught. That could take time."

Principal Ashcraft shook her head. "We can't afford to lose state funding. We barely get enough now to pay the staff and the utility bills."

"Principal Ashcraft..." the sheriff reached across the table for the principal's hand and held it in his big one, "Joyce, this alternative makes sense. The Brotherhood Protectors can provide you with alternative staffing and the protection your students and staff need until we can identify the attacker and bring him to justice. It will also give you time to find temporary replacements for your PE teacher and Mr. Jones."

Principal Ashcraft sighed, staring at her hand covered by Sheriff Bergeron's. "I know you're right. It's just that everything is happening so quickly, I can't wrap my head around it." She looked across into the sheriff's eyes. "Who would do such a thing to a junior high?"

"I don't know," the sheriff said. "But we intend to find out."

"At least he didn't attack during the school day," Deputy Taylor offered.

"Or with an automatic weapon," the sheriff added softly.

Valentin winced. What the sheriff said was true, but telling a school principal that harsh information might be a little too much, although Valentin suspected the sheriff had used the statement for its shock factor to get through to the principal.

Joyce Ashcraft blanched and pressed a hand to her mouth. "He's still out there. Who's to say he won't come back with that automatic weapon?"

"Our guys will basically be undercover," Remy said. "If the perpetrator returns, he won't know what he'll be up against."

Principal Ashcraft's frown deepened. "Wouldn't it be better to have somebody dressed in a police uniform as a visual deterrent to anyone who might consider attacking the junior high?"

"What exactly are you proposing?" Valentin asked.

Remy tipped his head toward Landry. "Landry will fill in for Mr. Jones, the janitor and work the night shift, keeping an eye on the school." The team lead smiled at Valentin. "I want you to fill in for Miss Sutton, the PE teacher."

Those eyebrows dipped low. "Me? A PE teacher to children?"

"That's right," Remy said.

Valentin clamped his lips shut to keep from arguing in front of the principal. He'd wait until she was out of earshot to tell Remy what he thought of the assignment.

"I wouldn't exactly call them children," Principal Ashcraft said. "They are young ladies and gentlemen ages thirteen through fifteen. They might take offense to being called children." She drew a breath and let it out slowly. "Okay then, I guess I don't have much choice. I can't close the school, and I can't risk the lives of my students and staff." Her brow puckered. "Having the Brotherhood Protectors on campus would make it a safer place. However, did you understand when I said we don't have enough budget to pay the utilities and the staff? How are we going to pay your team?"

Remy gave the principal a gentle smile. "We don't offer our protection solely to people who can pay. Our founders, Hank Patterson and Sadie McClain, have picked up the tab on a number of occasions."

"Well, I guess that settles it then." Principal Ashcraft pushed to her feet. When all the men at the table started to rise, she held up her hands. "Please stay seated. I'm sure you have more to talk about. Thank you for coming to our assistance. Now, if you will excuse me, I need to get ready. I meet with the president of the PTA next. I'm sure she will coordinate a volunteer effort to get the classroom cleaned up and ready for school as usual on Monday."

Remy nodded. "Members of our team will be here to help set things to rights and clean and paint."

The principal left the conference room.

When the sheriff stood, Deputy Taylor did as well. Remy, Landry and Valentin all stood as one.

"I'm on duty," Deputy Taylor said, "or I would stay and help."

"I'll be here," Sheriff Bergeron said, "after I go home and change out of this monkey suit. We don't have the budget to replace uniforms due to paint splatter." He gave the others a mock salute and left the room.

Remy handed a sheet of paper to Valentin. "This is your class schedule for the week. You might want to memorize it."

Valentin followed Remy out to the hall, determined to rectify this bogus assignment. "I know you've heard me say this before, and believe me, it's no secret—I left the Navy to avoid teaching new BUD/S recruits, kids who are wet behind the ears. I know nothing about children. I was an only child. Practically an adult since birth." Valentin turned to Landry. "You had siblings, didn't you?"

Landry grinned. "We were stairstep children, all fourteen months apart. We gave our parents hell from the ages of 12 through 18." His grin widened. "I can't think of a better person to fill in as a PE teacher than you." The man had the audacity to chuckle. "Consider it a learning experience. I bet those kids have more to teach you than you have to teach them."

Valentin snorted in disgust and turned back to Remy. "I'd be more suited as the janitor than PE teacher," Valentin said. "Landry would be much better equipped to lead young teens in hopscotch and kickball than I would."

Remy shook his head. "It's settled. Valentin. You'll fill in as the PE teacher. Landry will take up where Mr. Jones left off as the janitor. Your new duties begin Monday, an hour before the first bell rings. And Valentin, you might want to brush up on activities for the gifted and talented. Miss Sutton was not only the PE teacher but also led the gifted and talented class."

Valentin groaned. "Is it too late to hand in my resignation?" he asked, knowing the answer.

"That ship sailed when you signed on with the Bayou Brotherhood Protectors, vowing to take on any assignment no matter how big or small." Remy grinned.

Holy hell, he was stuck. Valentin shoved a hand through his hair, wondering why he'd signed on as a Brotherhood Protector.

Remy's gleeful smirk stuck in Valentin's craw, making him grumpier than sleep deprivation could count for.

His team lead clapped his hands together. "Lucas and Beau are at the hardware store picking up paint, brushes, rollers and drop cloths. Gerard is borrowing brooms, dust pans and mops from Broussard's General Store. Hank is arranging for a glass company out of New Orleans to make a special trip today to replace the broken window. Our team is scheduled to converge on the damaged classroom in forty-five minutes. You need to go change into old clothes you don't mind getting paint on and get back here in time to get to work."

Valentin grumbled beneath his breath, "I don't even like kids."

"Maybe not but let me show you what we're dealing with." Remy turned to the right and strode down a long corridor, stopping in front of one door. He waved a hand toward the room. "See for yourself.

Valentin and Landry entered the room.

Landry let out a low whistle. "Wow. It looks like this place was struck by a tornado."

He was right. Every desk either lay on its side or upside down. Some desktops were broken. Metal legs were bent at odd angles. Plastic seats were destroyed. The whiteboard had been ripped off the wall, along with posters depicting the periodic table and diagrams of the bones, muscles, tendons and ligaments in the body.

Bold red paint had been sprayed across the walls, forming vicious, threatening statements.

EVOLUTION IS BLASPHEMY

MIZ MO THE HO

SAY NO TO SEX ED

DIE BITCH!

LEAVE OR DIE!

"Did the student and science teacher see this?" Valentin said quietly.

"Yes," Remy answered behind him.

"That's not just destruction of property," Valentin said. "Those are real threats. Is anyone watching out for the science teacher at this time?"

"Shelby's on her way to Miss Maudet's cottage as we speak," Remy said. "They had a unit cruise by her place several times during the night."

"Is that enough?" Valentin asked.

"Not as far as I can tell." Remy stepped up beside Valentin. "From what Shelby says, she's pretty independent and would resist having a bodyguard assigned. That's where you come in. Befriend her. Get close. She may not think she needs someone looking out for her, but she does."

"Then why not just assign me as her bodyguard? Why all the pretense of being a PE teacher?" Valentin asked.

"Shelby and the sheriff thought it best that the school, the students and the staff remain unaware that the people replacing the PE teacher, and the janitor are there to look after them. Most importantly, we don't want the vandal to know that you'll be watching for him. He has to be a member of the community. He knew Miss Maudet was the science teacher and that she has Darwinism and sex education as part of her curriculum. Plus, he knew exactly which room he was vandalizing."

Valentin felt sorry for the old teacher. It was hard enough to teach teenagers. To be attacked so viciously might screw with her mental health.

Remy turned to Valentin. "So, now that you've seen the damage, do you still want to submit your resignation?"

Valentin sighed. "No. But I still think Landry would be the better PE teacher."

"So noted." Remy glanced down at his watch. "You

have forty minutes to change and be back here. Something else you might want to consider is that the whole community might show up to help with the cleanup effort. That might include the students and teachers. I'll be introducing you two as the replacement PE teacher and janitor to get the ball rolling."

Great. Valentin was truly stuck as the PE teacher. He walked with Landry out of the building, making a beeline for his truck.

Landry followed and clapped a hand on Valentin's back. "Congratulations, old man. I can't wait to see the reactions on your students' faces when you drop them for push-ups."

"Shut up," Valentin snarled. "You'll be too busy scrubbing toilets and prying gum from beneath desktops to see the students' reactions."

Landry smile faded. "Can't be any worse than scrubbing latrines in basic training." He frowned. "On second thought, I remember how gross the bathrooms were when I was in school. If I thought there was any chance of swapping jobs, I'd appeal to Remy in a heartbeat." Landry's grin reappeared. "Then you could scrub all the toilets and the dried gum."

"I'm barely good with adults," Valentin said. "I know nothing about teens."

"They like it when you speak to them like they're adults," Landry said. "Boys can be pigheaded, and they do stupid shit. Girls are more mature but are also hormonal drama queens who cry about everything. It's like navigating a minefield. You'll do great." Landry laughed all the way to his SUV.

The twenty minutes it took to get from the school to the boarding house and back wasn't nearly enough time for Valentin to come to grips with this assignment.

In that short amount of time, the parking lot had filled with cars, trucks and people.

Out of parking spaces, Valentin pulled his truck into a grassy field adjacent to the parking lot and shifted into park. He didn't much like crowds. The people streaming into the small school were more than enough to make him want to shift to drive, go to the marina and rent a boat to drive far out into the bayou.

Valentin sighed. He'd had to do a lot of things in his life that he hadn't really wanted to do. This was no different. And the damaged classroom needed to be set to rights before the kids returned to school on Monday. They didn't need to see the damning words spray-painted in red across the wall.

Another truck pulled up beside his. Beau Boyette pushed open the driver's door and dropped to the ground. "Hey, Valentin, wanna give us a hand?"

"Sure," he said and hurried over to grab the four cans of paint Beau handed him from the truck bed.

Beau retrieved four more cans of paint.

Lucas climbed out of the passenger seat carrying a box filled with paint brushes, roller trays, rolls of masking tape and clear plastic sheeting to use as a drop cloth.

"How many classrooms are you planning on painting?" Valentin asked.

Beau's lips twisted into a wry grin. "I wasn't sure how many coats it would take to cover bright red spray paint. Rather too much than too little. They want to finish today."

Another truck parked beside Valentin's. Gerard Guidry and Alan Broussard got out and gathered brooms, mops, dustpans and a tool bag from the truck bed.

Lucas fell in step beside Valentin. "Looks like we have more than enough help to make quick work of this job."

"Too much, if you ask me," Valentin groused.

Lucas laughed. "I hear you got tagged with the assignment." The man shook his head. "I'm having a hard time imagining you as a PE teacher." He tilted his head. "No. On second thought, I can see those teens doing pushups, sit-ups and running laps around you in no time."

Valentin didn't bother to rise to Lucas's taunts.

When the men and woman standing near the door saw the men carrying supplies, they parted and let them through.

The two passed through the main entrance and

turned left. A couple of men came out of the damaged classroom carrying a destroyed desk.

"I take it that's the classroom we'll be working in?" Lucas asked.

Valentin nodded. "That's the one."

Lucas peered into one of the classrooms as he passed. "Shouldn't take too long if that room is anything like these."

"They're all pretty much the same size," Valentin said.

They were two doors away when a loud crash was followed by screams emanating from the classroom where they were headed. Women and men scrambled through the doorway out to the hall.

"Oh my God," one woman screeched. "Did you kill him? Please tell me you killed him." She moved further down the hall, dancing nervously on her toes while staring down at the tiled floor.

The man beside her shook his head, his gaze also on the floor, his knees bent, ready to run. "I'm not touching him barehanded."

"Don't you have a gun?" the woman asked.

"Not on me," the man said. "It's out in my truck."

"Well, don't just stand there. Go get it," the woman demanded. "Miz Mo is in there. She could be hurt."

Valentin quickly set the paint cans on the floor and hurried to the open classroom door. He eased around the door frame and stared into the room.

Many of the desks had already been moved toward the center of the room. Glass from the broken window still littered the floor. The big white-board leaned against a wall behind the metal teacher's desk. A pair of shoes poked out from one end of the whiteboard and suddenly disappeared.

"Give it up, Houdini," a female voice said from behind the whiteboard. "Either you come with me, or someone is going to kill you," she warned. Then softly, she said, "That's it. Stay still. Just a few more inches… Gotcha!"

The big whiteboard shimmied and then fell with a loud crash, exposing the female behind it, her shapely ass in the air, elbows on the ground and something caught between her fingers. Whatever it was wiggled loose and escaped her grasp.

She lunged after it, missed, and it slid beneath ragged wads of poster paper and under the desk.

"Don't just stand there," the woman yelled, "catch him." On her hands and knees, she scrambled toward the desk.

Valentin lunged across the room and dropped down on his knees in front of the desk. He lowered his head to peer beneath, only to find himself face-to-face with a snake. But not just any snake. This one reared up and spread its neck like a goddamn cobra.

"What the hell?" he uttered.

"Catch him," the woman called out from the other side of the desk.

"You've got to be kidding," Valentin said, scooting back on the floor. "It's a cobra."

"Oh, for the love of—" The woman dove beneath the desk, snagged the snake by its tail and pulled it toward her.

"Careful, lady, it might bite you." Valentin grabbed a nearby dustpan and shot to his feet. He held the dustpan like a shield and rounded the desk toward the woman.

She rose with her hand gripping the snake firmly, the creature's body looped around her arm.

"Relax, Sir Galahad," she said, her voice dripping with sarcasm. "Cobras are not native to the United States. But Hognose Spreading Adders are." She held up her arm with a snake. "Meet the classroom snake, Houdini, named for his innate ability to escape his living quarters."

"You keep a snake in a classroom?" Valentin fought the urge to shiver. He could understand keeping a gerbil, a mouse or a bird in the classroom. But a snake?

The woman lifted her chin, her dark auburn hair bounced around her shoulders, and her green eyes flashed. "I want my students to understand that all snakes are not evil. For instance, the Hognose Spreading Adder is harmless."

"Does he bite?" Valentin asked.

"Only in self-defense. The hognose would rather bluff his way out of a difficult situation by playing dead. He'll roll over and expose his white belly, hoping his attacker will move on." Her empty hand stroked the snake's body.

Valentin did shiver this time.

She frowned. "Let me guess… You're one of those people who consider the only good snake is a dead snake. Am I right?"

Valentin nodded. "You got that right."

"That's too bad," she said. "I thought there might be hope for you when you didn't run from the room like the rest of them." She held Houdini out toward him. "Perhaps you just haven't met the right snake. Maybe if you hold him for a minute, you'll see snakes aren't slimy as most people assume. They're interesting."

Valentin held up his hands. "You seemed to have a good hold on him. I would hate to fumble and have him escape again."

The woman's pretty lips twisted in a wry grin. "Perhaps you're right. He's already been traumatized enough. He had a little help with his escape this time when the vandal dropped the terrarium on the floor, shattering it into a million pieces. Houdini's lucky he wasn't severely injured. I'm just glad we found him. He's lived most of his life in captivity and wouldn't know what to do in the wild." She faced the snake and smiled gently. "Isn't that right, sweetie? You have it pretty cushy here in my classroom."

Valentin frowned. "Your classroom?"

Her dark red eyebrows winged upward. "That's right. This is my classroom." She glanced around, her mouth pressing into a tight line. When she turned back to him, she held out her empty hand. "I'm Ouida Mae Maudet, but the students all call me Miz Mo. And you are?"

"Stunned," Valentin said without thinking, taking her hand in his. An electric shock zipped through his nervous system. "You're the science teacher?"

She gave him a tight smile. "Guilty. Why? What did you expect?"

"Nothing," he backpaddled quickly. "It's just that you're nothing like the science teacher I had in junior high."

"Yeah, well, I am qualified to teach, or so it says on my diplomas." She tilted her head. "You still haven't told me who you are." Her gaze went to where his hand still held hers. "And that's my hand. I'd kind of like to have it back."

"Sorry." He immediately released her hand, and heat rose up his neck into his cheeks. "I'm the new...PE teacher, filling in for Miss Sutton." He didn't add *and here to keep an eye on you and your students.*

Staring down into her pretty green eyes, a part of him thought this assignment might not be as bad as he'd originally expected.

Keeping an eye on the pretty science teacher would be no problem at all.

Miz Mo cocked a challenging eyebrow. "How

much experience do you have working with junior high students?"

Valentin held up his hands. "None. It's all new territory for me." He grimaced. "How hard could it be?"

CHAPTER 3

OUIDA MAE LAUGHED OUT LOUD, her gaze sweeping over her new coworker. He was tall, broad-shouldered and athletic-looking, with a neatly trimmed beard that gave him a slightly dangerous appeal. That might help to intimidate the teenagers he would be working with, perhaps enough to keep them in line. But the man was clueless.

She could warn him all day long about the difficulties of working with hormonal teenagers, but, in this case, experience was the only way to learn.

She grinned. "Well, it's nice to meet you. Welcome to Bayou Mambaloa Junior High, and good luck."

His dark brow dipped, adorably confused. "Thanks…?"

A man Ouida Mae recognized stepped through the door, carrying a box full of paint supplies. "Everything all right in here?"

"Yes," Ouida Mae responded. "Everything is as well as could be expected." She smiled. "You're Lucas, Felina's fiancé, right?"

Lucas nodded. "That's me. And you must be Felina's friend, Ouida Mae, the science teacher. Or should I call you Miz Mo?"

"I'll answer to either," she said.

"Then I'll call you Ouida Mae since Felina called you that, and you're not my teacher. Although, I might've been a better student if you had been." He set the box of supplies on her desk and held out a hand. "Lucas LeBlanc at your service."

"Nice to finally meet you," Ouida Mae said. "And congratulations on your engagement."

"Thank you," he said. "I'm a lucky man. She actually said yes." He glanced around the room and let out a low whistle. "Looks like we have our work cut out for us. We're on painting detail."

Ouida Mae looked from Lucas to Valentin. "You know each other?"

"Yes, ma'am," Lucas said.

Valentin's elbow connected with Lucas's belly. "Lucas and I worked together after we both left the military."

"Are you part of that group of men who came to town about the same time Remy Montagne appeared?" Ouida Mae's brow dipped. "What was it Felina called you? Some kind of brotherhood?"

"Bayou Brotherhood Protectors," Lucas said.

"What is that...some kind of bodyguard work?" she asked.

Lucas shoved a hand through his hair. "Yes, ma'am. Something like that."

"Is that why all those men came to Bayou Mambaloa?" Ouida Mae turned to Valentin and raised an eyebrow. "Is that why *you* came?"

Valentin hesitated and then nodded. "Yes, ma'am."

She shook her head. Was he nuts? "That sounds a lot more interesting than teaching junior high students."

Valentin shrugged. "Business has been a bit slow. I was looking for something to fill the time."

She stared at the big, former military guy. "You couldn't get on at the hardware store or help the Broussards with the general store?"

"I heard Principal Ashcraft was in a tight spot, needed a substitute PE teacher and that it was a temporary position until she could get a permanent replacement. My buddy Landry volunteered to help out until the janitor recovers."

Lucas clapped Valentin on the back. "That's right. Community service at its best."

Ouida Mae looked from the new PE teacher to Lucas and back. Something about their story didn't sit right with her.

Mr. Garner, the Math teacher, stuck his head in the door. "Did you kill it?"

Ouida Mae held the arm up with the snake

wrapped around it. "Of course I didn't," she said. "You know Houdini is the classroom mascot."

Mr. Garner frowned. "Couldn't you have chosen a bunny or a gerbil, instead?"

"Snakes are more interesting," Ouida Mae said. "Anyway, he's not a threat to you. I just need to get him a new home since his terrarium was destroyed in the attack." She marched past Mr. Garner.

The math teacher backed away, his hands held up as if warding off a curse.

"Don't worry, Mr. Garner," Ouida Mae said. "Houdini is just as scared as you are." She headed for the teachers' lounge, where she knew of an old aquarium stored in a closet that wasn't being used. She hoped it still had a lid, otherwise it wouldn't keep Houdini in for long. She felt bad that she hadn't looked for the snake sooner. The incident had shaken her so much she hadn't been thinking straight.

Once she found the aquarium, she placed Houdini inside. Thankfully, the lid was still intact. She placed it over the top. "We'll make you more comfortable once we get the classroom in order," she promised.

Ouida Mae carried the aquarium back to the classroom, where she placed it in the middle of her desk, out of the way of the people sweeping up glass and spreading plastic sheeting around the room. While she pretended to adjust the aquarium's position, her gaze went to the new PE teacher as he applied masking tape around the top of the door frame, his arms stretching high, the muscles rippling in his biceps.

No doubt, the man would be a distraction to all the single female teachers as well as the married ones. Already, he was a distraction to her. She shook her head as if that would clear her mind of the man. It didn't.

And she didn't have time for a distraction. Her classroom needed to be up and running by Monday morning when the students returned to school.

Lucas held up a roller and a paintbrush. "Choose your weapon."

"I'll take the roller," she said. "The sooner the red spray paint is covered, the better."

Lucas tipped his head toward two other men who were busy taping off the windowsills. "Those two boneheads are part of our team. The tall one's Gerard. The other guy is Beau." Lucas raised his voice. "Guys, say hello to the science teacher, Ouida Mae."

Gerard and Beau glanced her way.

"You're the science teacher?" Beau asked, his eyebrows rising.

Ouida Mae waved at the two. "That's me."

"I might've been more interested in science if I'd had a teacher like you," Beau said.

Gerard tossed his roll of masking tape at Beau. "Better not let the senator's daughter hear you say that."

"Aurelie knows I love her to the moon and back," Beau said and waved at Ouida Mae. "Nice to meet you, Miss Ouida Mae."

"The students call her Miz Mo," Lucas said.

"And you're okay with that?" Gerard asked.

Ouida Mae smiled and dipped her roller into a pan of soft French gray paint. "Absolutely."

"Pretty and nice," Valentin said behind her.

At the sound of Valentin's voice so close behind her, Ouida Mae spun, forgetting she had a wet roller in her hand.

Paint slung across the plastic sheeting and Valentin's faded Def Leppard T-shirt.

"Oh, I'm so sorry," Ouida Mae reached out to wipe the paint from his shirt, only managing to smear it over the faces of the band members.

Valentin captured her wrist in his big, warm hand. "It's okay."

"No, it's not," she cried. "Maybe I can rinse it out before it dries." She set the roller down in the pan and reached for the hem of Valentin's shirt. "Take it off."

"Yes, please," a female voice called out behind her.

"Yeah. Take it off," another said.

While she'd been focused on the men in her room, Ouida Mae's fellow teachers had entered.

"Take it off. Take it off. Take it off," they all chanted as one.

Lucas laughed. "Do it, Valentin."

Ouida Mae's hands were halfway up Valentin's chest when another voice sounded from the doorway.

"What's going on?" Principal Ashcraft stood in the doorway, her arms crossed over her chest.

Ouida Mae's paint-splattered hands fell to her sides. Heat burned in her cheeks.

"Ah, Principal Ashcraft." Valentin gave a brief smile. "Miz Mo was just helping me get some paint out of my shirt before it dried." He grabbed the hem of his shirt and yanked it up over his head, managing to get paint in his beard and hair. He held out the shirt to Ouida Mae. "Do you really think you can get the paint out? It's my lucky shirt."

Her cheeks still hot, Ouida Mae nodded.

Principal Ashcraft's brow puckered. "Mr. Vachon, Ms. Maudet can show you where to find the teachers' lounge, where you can work on getting the paint out of your beard and hair, too."

Donna Durand, the tall and wispy-thin English teacher, raised a hand. "I could show Mr. Vachon to the teacher's lounge."

Principal Ashcraft's lips pressed together in a tight line. "That won't be necessary. Miz Mo is headed there anyway, aren't you?"

"Yes, ma'am," Ouida Mae choked out. "Follow me," she said to Valentin.

He murmured something that sounded suspiciously like *to the ends of the earth.*

Ouida Mae chalked it up to her addled brain. How had the new PE teacher reduced her scientific, logical mind to muddled mush in less than thirty minutes of knowing him?

As she passed her friend and coworker, Donna, the other woman muttered, "Lucky dog."

Lucky? Was she crazy? The last thing Ouida Mae needed was more time in the man's presence. She had enough problems with the vandal who'd destroyed her classroom.

She didn't wait to see if the man followed her but took off at a quick pace toward the office.

She'd almost reached it when Katherine Edouard stepped through the front entrance, dressed in a neatly pressed white painter's jumpsuit, her hair tied back with a colorful scarf and makeup expertly applied.

As the wife of a local politician, President of the Parent Teacher Association, Sunday school teacher and mother of the junior high's star quarterback, Ms. Edouard called a lot of the shots at the school and in the community. She liked being in charge and leading protests against things she deemed unacceptable.

She'd been in discussions with Principal Ashcraft, trying to put a stop to Ouida Mae's sex education curriculum, even though parents had the right to opt out of the instruction for their students. She didn't think any student should be subjected to the instruction, claiming it would lead to promiscuity in teens too young to understand the risks.

When Ms. Edouard spotted Ouida Mae, she advanced on her, a scowl marring her perfect face. "Well, I can't say I'm surprised your room was targeted. It appears I'm not the only member of this community gravely concerned about what you're teaching our children. Whoever trashed your class just took it a step further. Maybe now, you'll pull sex education and evolution from your syllabus."

The stress and worry weighing down on Ouida Mae bubbled up into anger. "You condone the vandal's actions?"

"Of course not." Ms. Edouard lifted her chin and stared down her nose at Ouida Mae, taking complete advantage of her superior height. "But it did get the message across."

"He almost killed Mr. Jones." Ouida Mae drew herself up to her full five feet two inches and stood toe to toe with the other woman. "Was Mr. Jones's life worth *getting the message across?*"

Katherine Edouard took a step back, her lip lifting on one side. "You're being overly dramatic. Mr. Jones is an old man who should've retired years ago. How do you know he didn't just trip and fall?"

Ouida Mae tamped down her rage. It was wasted on someone like Katherine Edouard. She couldn't see any other point of view that wasn't her own. "I know he didn't fall because I was there. Now, if you will excuse me, I have a classroom to clean up so I can teach my sex ed curriculum on Monday." Ouida Mae stepped around the woman.

Ms. Edouard grabbed Ouida Mae's arm. "Seriously? You're still going through with that lesson plan?"

"Yes, ma'am."

Valentin stepped closer. "Please release Ms. Maudet's arm."

The woman retained her hold and glared up at Valentin. "Who the hell are you? Miz Mo's shirtless bodyguard?"

Valentin shook his head. "No, ma'am. I'm the new PE teacher. Now, release Ms. Maudet's arm."

"Or what?" Ms. Edouard challenged.

"Or this," Ouida Mae said, tired to the bone of the woman's high-handedness. Ouida Mae grabbed the woman's wrist, stepped to her side and twisted her arm up and behind her back, pressing the wrist up between the self-righteous bitch's shoulder blades.

"You're hurting me," Ms. Edouard said. "I could have you fired for attacking me."

"The way I saw it, you attacked Ms. Maudet," Valentin said with a dangerous smile. "She could file assault charges against you."

"Don't. Ever. Touch. Me. Again," Ouida Mae said into Ms. Edouard's ear before giving her a slight shove at the same time as she released the woman's wrist.

Katherine Edouard straightened, rubbing her wrist. "I'm not done with this conversation."

"I am." Ouida Mae passed the woman and continued toward the office and the teacher's lounge.

"I will not have you teaching my impressionable young son how to have sex," Katherine called out.

Ouida Mae stopped and turned back. "I'm not teaching anyone *how* to have sex. Most likely, he already knows that. If you think otherwise, you're burying your head in the sand. I teach them what can happen if they do have sex—the consequences of unprotected sex, like sexually transmitted diseases and pregnancy. I also teach them that *no* means *no*. Young men and women don't always get that information from their parents. Have you explained any of that to Chase?"

Ms. Edouard's lips curled. "I will when he's ready."

"Lady," Valentin said, "at his age, he's dangerously past the ready mark."

"You don't know my son like I do," the parent said.

"I was a teenage boy. I knew about sex before I got pubic hair. Kids need to know what can happen *after sex* to help make better decisions *before* engaging in it, to include abstinence."

"I care about my students," Ouida Mae added. "My goal is to keep them safe from disease and teen pregnancy."

"Well, none of that will happen to my son,"

Katherine said, "because you won't be putting those ideas into his head."

Ouida Mae's eyes narrowed. "Then make sure he comes to school Monday with the form I sent home with him, with your signature and the box checked indicating you do not wish your child to receive the sex education instruction."

"What form?" Katherine demanded.

"You know your son; ask him." Ouida Mae turned and walked away.

Valentin followed. "Are all parents like that one?"

"Thankfully, no." Ouida Mae passed the office and pushed through the next door marked TEACHERS ONLY.

Still amped up from her encounter with the sanctimonious Edouard woman, Ouida Mae couldn't look at Valentin. Anger was a passion of its own. Gazing at Valentin's naked chest might unleash that passion in a very different and frightening way. For a science teacher who valued logic and strict control of her emotions, the new PE teacher was a real threat.

With the paint-stained shirt still clutched in her hand, she weaved her way through the tables and chairs to the kitchen sink on the far side of the room.

"There are school T-shirts in the cabinet to the right of the copy machine. Find one your size, my treat."

She didn't wait for a response but found the plug

for the drain and filled the sink with warm, soapy water. After dunking the shirt in and out several times, she rubbed the fabric together, working the paint out a little at a time. The repetitive motion and strenuous rubbing also eased some of the tension from her body.

"Mind if I get some of that soap and water?" Valentin's deep voice said so close Ouida Mae felt the warmth of his breath against her ear.

She jumped, dropping the shirt into the suds.

"Preferably before the paint sets in my beard and hair," Valentin added.

Ouida Mae glanced up in time to catch his grin and a wink.

Her knees wobbled, and her heart skipped several beats and then thumped hard against her ribs. The man was close enough that all she had to do was raise her hand, and her fingers would graze his naked, muscular chest.

His brow furrowed. "Sorry. Did I startle you? I tried to get your attention, but you were rubbing that shirt so hard, I'm betting there won't be much left of it." His smile was back.

"Couldn't you find a shirt?" She winced at how breathy her voice sounded.

He held up a T-shirt with the school logo.

"Didn't want to put it on until I've got the paint out of my hair."

"Oh, right." She had to force her gaze upward

from the broad expanse of his chest to the splash of French gray paint in his beard.

Ouida Mae had always wondered how it felt to kiss a man with a beard. Would it tickle? If he went down on her, would it send tingles throughout her body?

Hell. Just the thought of him going down on her sent tingles. Beard or no beard.

His lips quirked. "If I had a mirror, I'd do it myself. If you could point the way to the bathroom, that would help."

She swallowed hard and fought for a grip. "That won't be necessary," she managed. "I'll get the paint out. It was my fault to begin with."

She snatched a paper towel from the roll beside the sink, dipped it into the soapy water and turned back to Valentin, his naked chest and that neatly trimmed, tempting beard. She was doomed before she started.

CHAPTER 4

VALENTIN'S PULSE was already racing before the pretty little science teacher faced him with the damp paper towel.

Her gaze landed on his chest first, pushing his heartrate even faster. When she raised her gaze to his chin, her tongue darted out and swept across lush, rosy lips.

Valentin swallowed hard with a groan. He'd never been so tempted to kiss a woman as he was at that moment. He wouldn't have far to go. She was so close he could feel the heat radiating off her body.

Or was that his heat? God, he was on fire.

She reached up, her elbow brushing against his bare chest, sending a spark of electricity ripping through his entire body and sending signals south. His groin tightened. If she got much closer, she'd soon discover just how much effect she had on him.

Ouida Mae touched the damp paper towel to his beard and gently wiped at the paint. "It's not coming off with water." Reaching up with her other hand, she captured some of the hairs in his beard between her fingernails and pulled them to the end of the short strand.

"There." She smiled briefly. "Got that bit. I forgot how bristly a man's beard felt."

A stab of something sharp pierced Valentin's chest. Something that felt a lot like...jealousy?

No way.

But when he thought of the petite teacher running her fingers through another man's beard, his gut clenched. "An old boyfriend?" he asked, not that he had the right to know.

She laughed. "My first boyfriend, when I was four years old."

He blinked. "A four-year-old with a beard?"

Ouida Mae shook her head. "No. My grandfather. He pretended to be my boyfriend and took me on my first date. He wanted to set the bar for my expectations of future dates."

"Smart man." Valentin could picture a tiny, redheaded four-year-old with a name bigger than herself, all dressed up to go out with her grandfather.

The mental image almost made him reconsider his moratorium on children of his own. He'd want to continue Ouida Mae's grandfather's tradition of taking his granddaughter or daughter out on her first date. It was quaint, and something every good father should do to set the example of how a man should treat a woman.

"If you'll have a seat, I'll get the paint out of your hair." Ouida Mae waved toward one of the metal and plastic chairs placed around the tables.

Though he was perfectly capable of getting the paint out himself, he obediently pulled a chair out and sat.

Ouida Mae stepped up in front of him, her knees brushing against his. "Lean your head forward," she instructed.

Standing, Val was at least a foot taller than the science teacher. Seated, his gaze was eye-level with her breasts. Tipping his head forward, even slightly, gave him a view into the cleavage of her button-up blouse.

If he were a gentleman, he would close his eyes. No matter how quaint and morally correct her story of her grandfather setting the bar was, Val couldn't resist studying the gentle swell of feminine skin and the taunting peek of a lacey pink bra. The science teacher had a saucy, feminine side Valentin wanted to explore.

While Ouida Mae scraped her fingernails across strands of Val's hair, he sat on his hands to keep from reaching out and resting them on her hips.

"Just a little bit more," Ouida Mae said.

Val opened his mouth to tell her she'd done enough. His cock strained against his denim jeans, making him very uncomfortable. If she didn't step back soon, he'd physically set her back and hurry from the room before she saw the raging evidence of his desire.

"Ouida Mae!" a voice called out across the room. "Thank the mother, you're all right."

Val glanced up as a small young woman with long, wavy dark hair and exotic coloring sailed into the room.

He smiled when he recognized his teammate Rafael's wife, Gisele, who happened to be the granddaughter of the local Voodoo queen. He'd been at their unusual outdoor wedding with Johnny, Gisele's pet Macaw, in attendance.

Gisele ground to stop in front of Ouida Mae and flung her arms around her. "Rafael and I just got back from New Orleans when I heard what happened here yesterday. I can't believe your classroom was attacked. Are you okay?" She leaned back, her gaze sweeping over Ouida Mae. "Did he hurt you? I heard about Jonesy. I hope he's all right. I heard they transferred him to New Orleans last night. Had I known, I would've stopped by before heading back to Bayou Mambaloa. Talk to me. What happened?"

Ouida Mae laughed. "I'll tell you as soon as you let me."

"I was just so worried." Gisele drew in a deep breath and let it out slowly. "I'll be quiet now. Tell all."

Ouida Mae gave Gisele the short version of the story.

Gisele shook her head. "Wow. That's scary. I'm glad he didn't come after you or your student. And what's with all the vehicles in the parking lot?"

Ouida Mae smiled. "A lot of people showed up to help put my classroom back together before school on Monday morning."

Her friend's eyebrows rose as she glanced toward Valentin. "Why are you two here instead of in your room?"

Ouida Mae's cheeks blossomed pink. "I got paint in Valentin's hair." She tipped her head toward Valentin. "But I got the majority of it out. You can put on the shirt now," she said to him. "I'll wring out your other shirt and put it through my washer this evening. I can get it back to you on Monday when you come to work."

"What do you mean when he comes to work on Monday?" Gisele asked. "Did you hire him as a bodyguard?"

Ouida Mae quickly shook her head. "No. Principal Ashcraft hired him as a PE teacher, Misty Sutton's temporary replacement. Misty won't return to work until the attacker is captured and put away."

Gisele grimaced. "Seems a bit like overkill, if you

ask me." She gave Valentin a wry grin. "Hey, Valentin."

"Good to see the newlyweds are back in town," he said. "Who was keeping Johnny company while you and Rafael were in New Orleans?"

"Lena, my part-time assistant, takes care of Johnny when I'm not there," Gisele said.

Valentin grinned. "I heard Rafael taught Johnny some new words."

"Yes, he did." Gisele's lips pressed together. "Every time I walk into the shop, Johnny gives me a wolf whistle and says *sexy mama.*"

Ouida Mae laughed. "You're kidding."

"I wish I were." Gisele's disapproving frown turned upside down. "Although, it is kind of cute. Johnny took to Rafael from the beginning. He didn't bite him like he'd bite other men."

Valentin chuckled. "Glad to hear they're getting along."

Gisele's eyes narrowed. "Speaking of getting along..." Her gaze bounced from Ouida Mae to Valentin and back. "You seemed to be getting along really well before I interrupted. Anything I should know about?"

Ouida Mae's cheeks again filled with color. "No. We just met less than an hour ago."

"Love doesn't follow the clock," Gisele said, a sly smile curling the corners of her lips. "You've heard of love at first sight."

"Ha!" Valentin chuckled. "In our case, it would have been love at first snake sighting."

Ouida Mae's cheeks grew a deeper shade of pink. "Not that we're in love or anything. He helped me catch Houdini."

"A case of love me, love my snake?" Gisele teased.

"We're not in love," Ouida Mae insisted, her cheeks flaming red by then.

Valentin felt sorry for the petite science teacher. She'd been through enough. He opened his mouth to set the record straight, but Ouida Mae's friend beat him to it.

"Okay, okay." Gisele held up her hands. "I'll leave you two love birds to finish what you started."

Ouida Mae closed her eyes, her lips moving as if she were counting to ten.

"I'll be in your classroom with my sweetie," Gisele said. "Glad you're okay and your new PE teacher has you covered." She was halfway across the room when she stopped, turned and frowned. "I guess the poker game's off for tonight?"

Ouida Mae opened her eyes, her brow twisting. "Why would it be off?"

"Well, with everything that's happened, I would've thought you'd want some peace and quiet."

"Actually, I'm looking forward to the company," Ouida Mae said. "It's still on, if you can leave your new husband for a few hours."

"I'll be there," Gisele grinned. "With bells on my toes. I missed my girls."

Ouida Mae cocked an eyebrow. "Your new husband is going to let you out of his sight for a few hours?"

"He's got a date with his teammates at the Crawdad Hole." Gisele shot a glance toward Valentin.

"That's right," Valentin confirmed. "We have a team meeting there tonight. Although, poker night with the girls sounds like more fun."

Ouida Mae's eyes flared wide for a brief second before she said, "Sorry. We only have seating for six, and all are accounted for."

"Even if we had the room, men aren't allowed." Gisele sailed toward the exit. "It's just us girls. Where else can we talk about our guys?"

"If your poker game cancels, you could always come to the Crawdad Hole and hang with the team," Valentin offered. "We aren't exclusive." He shrugged. "I get wanting company after having your safe space attacked."

"Thanks," Ouida Mae said, as she twisted the T-shirt, wringing out the moisture. "I'll keep that in mind. But I'm sure the poker game will happen. It's our girl time. We've been doing it once a month for the past couple of years. It's become a tradition."

"It's nice to have close friends like that."

"One of the benefits of living in a small town."

Ouida Mae hung the T-shirt over the back of one of the chairs. "I'm ready to paint walls. How about you?"

"I'm ready." Gisele's timely arrival had given his body time to relax. He needed to get back to work with the guys before he had any more lustful thoughts about the pretty science teacher.

He waved a hand toward the door.

Ouida Mae led, and Valentin followed, once again, enjoying the sway of the teacher's hips.

By the time they entered the classroom, half the room had a full coat of paint. All the windows had been opened to allow fresh air in and paint fumes out.

"Love the T-shirt, Coach Vachon," Beau called out with a grin.

"Go Gators!" a tall, thin female called out.

Ouida Mae leaned toward Valentin and whispered. "That's Donna Durand, our English teacher. She's single if you're interested."

"Thanks, but I'm not into improving my English," he whispered back. "It wouldn't hurt to brush up on science, though."

"About time you got back to work." Beau handed Valentin a paintbrush. "You can take over on the corners and around the door frames. Landry and I will be checking over the desks."

Valentin went to work painting the hard-to-reach areas, while Ouida Mae spread wide swaths of paint over the walls, covering the angry red spray-painted messages like a woman on a mission.

When they had completed covering the walls in the soft gray color, they all stood back.

Ouida Mae sighed. "One coat isn't enough."

"She's right," Donna, the English teacher, agreed.

"Anyone hungry?" a voice called out from the hallway. A dark-haired, slightly plump young woman wearing a white apron and chef's hat appeared in the doorframe carrying a cardboard box.

Behind her was a tall dark-skinned woman dressed to the nines in a bright fuchsia skirt suit, matching high heels, with bold, shiny gold and silver bangles on her wrists and a chunky gold and silver necklace around her neck. Her fingernails were an inch and a half long and matched her pink, gold and silver outfit.

The chef gave the room full of volunteers a cheerful smile. "Lunch is on Baked with Love, and the beautiful, LaShawnda Jones." She entered and moved aside to allow the other woman in.

LaShawnda carried a large paper bag in one hand and rolled an ice chest on wheels into the room with the other.

While Valentin rushed forward to relieve the chef of the heavy box, Landry and Beau hurried to help LaShawnda with her items.

Ouida Mae hurried to hug the chef. "Ah, Amelie,

thank you so very much." She hugged the other woman. "And LaShawnda, you two are too kind."

LaShawnda patted Ouida Mae's back carefully and straightened. "I'm no good for painting, but I brought drinks and chips. Amelie brought the good stuff."

Amelie's cheeks flushed a pretty pink. "It's just sandwiches and cookies. The point is we all help where we can. So, please, eat up."

"Yes, please." LaShawnda patted her flat belly. "And don't leave a single cookie behind. My waistline can't afford it."

"That's very nice of you," Principal Ashcraft said. "You can make use of the faculty lounge if you'd like."

"Personally," Ouida Mae said, "I'd like to sit outside and soak up some sunshine."

"And fresh air," Valentin added.

"I'm all for fresh air," Landry pinched the bridge of his nose.

Ouida Mae frowned. "Will the paint fumes dissipate before Monday?"

"It would be best if we could leave the windows open and fans blowing air through them," Valentin said.

"Don't we have some big fans in the gym we could place in here over the weekend?" Ouida Mae asked the principal.

Ashcraft nodded. "We do."

"After we finish all we can do in here, our guys will move the fans into this classroom," Valentin said.

The principal frowned. "But that means we need to leave the windows open for the rest of the weekend."

Remy Montagne passed through the door into the classroom. "We can have our guys do shifts to keep an eye on the classroom until Monday morning."

"Oh, Mr. Montagne, you know the school can't afford to pay you," the principal said. "The Brotherhood Protectors have done so much already; I'd hate to ask for more."

"You don't have to ask." Remy glanced around the room. "Do I have any volunteers to set up guard duty for the rest of the weekend? I can take the midnight to six o'clock shift."

One by one, the other man of the Brotherhood Protectors raised a hand offering to fill another six-hour shift until all hours were accounted for until Monday morning. Valentin tried to take the last shift, sliding into the start of the school day on Monday.

"No way," Remy said. "You're going to need your wits about you come Monday morning and the students arrive."

"But—"

Remy raised a hand. "No buts. You'll need to be well-rested to manage a bunch of teenagers. They'll be extra everything, having a new PE teacher. You, my friend, are off the hook for guard duty."

Valentin didn't like that edict for two reasons, the first being that if his teammates had to pull guard duty, he felt that he should as well. Second, he didn't like that he had to consider the students as "extra."

Extra annoying.

Extra dramatic.

Extra hormonal.

Extra trying.

Extra hard to manage.

"Are some of us still on for the meeting at the Crawdad Hole?" Valentin asked. Though he'd rather play poker with the girls, one in particular, he could use some relaxation time with his friends.

"Damn right," Landry said. "I'm on duty at midnight. I'd like to catch a shrimp po'boy sandwich and a beer."

"I'm in," Landry said.

Beau raised a hand. "I'll be there."

"Since I'll be wifeless tonight," Rafael said, "I'll be there." He stood with his arm around Gisele's waist. "Although why she would think spending the evening with a bunch of women is preferable to being with her extremely handsome husband who loves her dearly….?" He puffed out his chest and angled his chin like a model for an aftershave commercial.

Gisele elbowed him in the ribs. "It's only a few hours. I'll be home before midnight."

Rafael leaned down and pressed a kiss to Gisele's

lips. "My mind will be consumed with you the entire time."

"Ha! I know you. Out of sight, out of mind." Gisele's lips twisted. "Your thoughts will be redirected by the burger and beer you'll consume with your buddies."

The loving smile Rafael gave Gisele tugged at Valentin's heart. He had never seen Rafael as happy as he was now that he'd found Gisele and convinced the independent business owner that he was the man for her.

Valentin had always shied away from commitment, much like Rafael had in the past. However, his friend had proven that it only took the right woman. Gisele was the right woman for Rafael.

Before he realized it, his gaze shifted toward the woman who had splattered paint on his beard. Was there a right woman for him?

Ouida Mae smiled at something Gisele said. Her glance shifted to him. When their gazes met, Ouida Mae's cheeks flushed a pretty pink, and her green eyes sparkled.

Yeah, Valentin would much rather go to the girls' poker night than drink beer with his buddies at the Crawdad Hole. He stood back while the volunteers and his teammates selected a sandwich, a drink, some of Amelie's famous cookies and headed outside.

He and Ouida Mae were the last two people left

in the classroom, with only one sandwich remaining in the box.

Ouida Mae chuckled. "You take it," she insisted. "I have food in the refrigerator in the teachers' lounge that I can eat."

"I wouldn't dream of it," he said. "You should have the sandwich. Besides, I'm trying to watch my girlish figure," he said with a smile. "And I'll be gorging on shrimp po'boys and fries this evening. It'll be a carb overload."

Ouida Mae smirked. "You don't have an ounce of fat on you. Girlish figure, my best Bunsen burner. There is nothing girlish about your figure."

Valentin's smile broadened. "So, you've been checking out my figure?"

Her cheeks flushed a pretty pink. "It's hard not to notice a man larger than life." She reached for the sandwich. "Tell you what, we can share the sandwich. It's too big for me to eat all of it anyway, and there are plenty of cookies left to fill us up."

"Deal," Valentin said. "Grab a drink; I'll grab the cookies."

They collected food and drinks and headed outside to the picnic benches near a sandpit with a volleyball net stretched across the center.

Ouida Mae found an empty space at the end of one of the picnic tables big enough for two and slid onto the bench.

Valentin dropped down beside her, his thigh

brushing against hers. That spark of awareness ignited the blood in his veins, sending it hot and fast southward to his groin.

Ouida Mae unwrapped the sandwich and spread the paper out. The sandwich had been cut in two, making it easy for them to share. She took the smaller half and pushed the other toward Valentin.

If the sandwich was good, Valentin wouldn't remember it. Not with his leg pressed against Ouida Mae's beneath the table. All he could think about was how warm and soft it was and how it would feel to have both of her legs wrapped around his waist.

Was it a bad thing to be having carnal thoughts about a woman on a school playground?

Principal Ashcraft emerged from a side door of the school carrying a volleyball. She had changed into leggings, a school T-shirt, and tennis shoes, making her appear more like one of her students than the principal. "Anyone for a game of volleyball?"

"I'm in," Landry called out.

"Me, too," Beau echoed.

Before long, all of Valentin's teammates were in the sand.

Ouida Mae consumed the last bite of her sandwich and dusted the crumbs off her fingertips. "Do you play?"

Valentin had finished his sandwich and was chewing on the last bite of his cookie. He swallowed. "I've played it a time or two."

"Then come on." Ouida Mae hopped out of her seat and hurried toward the sand court. "What's it to be? Guys against girls?"

LaShawnda held up her hands. "If I hadn't just had my nails done, I'd join you."

Ouida Mae grinned. "Not in that amazing outfit—nails or not."

LaShawnda gave her a crooked smile. "True. I have to show a house in an hour. You all play."

Valentin counted. "That's seven men to five women."

"We can take you," Principal Ashcraft said, bouncing the volleyball on her wrists.

"That's too many on our team," Remy said.

"Okay, then," Ouida Mae said, "we'll take the tall guy."

The man chuckled and herded Gerard to the other side of the net where the woman had taken positions, with Principal Ashcraft in place to serve first.

"First round as warmup," she called out and performed a neat underhanded serve.

Remy bumped the ball to Landry.

Landry set to Valentin.

Valentin hit an easy spike over the net to the back row consisting of the principal and the two shortest players, Ouida Mae and Gisele.

Ouida Mae bumped it to Amelie, who set to Gerard.

Gerard had never been the fastest or best when he played volleyball with the rest of his teammates, but he was the tallest. He easily spiked the ball straight down on the opposite side of the net.

Valentin dove and bumped the ball into the net. It bounced back at him. He ducked, and Beau set it to Landry, who went in for a killer spike. The ball landed outside the sand pit.

Donna Durand retrieved the ball and tossed it up and down in her hands. "Warm enough?"

Everyone nodded.

"Let the visiting team serve first," Principal Ashcraft said.

Donna tossed the ball to Remy. He performed an overhand serve, not too hard, not too soft. Gisele bumped, Ouida Mae set to Donna.

The tall, thin English teacher leaped into the air and spiked it.

Four of the six men on the other side of the court dove. The ball hit the sand in a gap between them.

Remy's brow wrinkled. "Fellas, I think we've been conned. Our opponents have some skills." He tossed the ball to Principal Ashcraft. The female team, plus Gerard, rotated.

Ouida Mae served a hard overhand that flew straight at Remy's head.

He ducked, apparently expecting it to fly outside the court. It skimmed over his head and dropped inside the boundary.

Valentin grinned.

No need to go easy on the "girls."

"Game on," he said softly but loud enough for his teammates to hear.

For the next thirty minutes, they played a rousing game of volleyball. The women won by three points.

"I'd say we let you win, but it would be a lie," Remy said as he shook hands with the principal. "Good game, Principal Ashcraft."

"Joyce," she corrected. "Thanks. Your guys were worthy opponents." She tipped her head toward Gerard. "And thanks for the added team member." She patted Gerard on his back. "You can play with us anytime."

"Good. I like being on a winning team," he said with a smirk.

"Traitor," Lucas called out.

"You have to admit my team was better looking than yours," Gerard said, a grin spreading across his face.

"He's not lying," Beau said.

Rafael stood beside Gisele, his arm encircling her waist. "Agreed. I'd play with them anytime, especially this one." He nuzzled Gisele's neck. She tipped her head up for a kiss.

"Come on, Romeo," Landry said, "we have another coat to apply before we can adjourn to the Crawdad Hole for an evening of beer, burgers and bullshit."

They gathered their trash and made their way back to the classroom.

Valentin caught up with Ouida Mae. "So, what's the scoop? Were we playing the Olympic sand volleyball team, or what?"

Ouida Mae laughed out loud. "Of course not. However, Principal Ashcraft did play a starting position on her college team, as did Donna. Gisele, Amelie and I played competitively on the Bayou Mambaloa High School team. We took it all the way to State and won the State Championship in my senior year."

By the time the guys finished painting and setting the usable desks and chairs in place, the ladies had tacked up informational posters like the periodic table, the different layers of the earth's crust and muscles, tendons and bones of a human body. The whiteboard had been scrubbed clean and rehung in its place on the wall behind Ouida Mae's desk. Her metal desk had been stripped of red spray paint and moved back in position.

The glass man had been and gone, replacing the broken window with a fresh, clean pane.

Ouida Mae stood at the door. The tears welling in her eyes worried Valentin.

"Did we get it right? Is there something still out of whack?"

She shook her head. "Not at all. Everything is perfect. Even better than before the incident."

"Then why the tears?" he asked.

"Other than Sophie, none of the other students have to see the horrible words that were spray-painted on the walls." She looked up at Valentin with a watery smile and then around the room at the other. "Thanks to you, your team and the ladies who helped make this happen, I can resume teaching where I left off on Friday as if nothing happened."

The men had positioned the fans in the room and were about to turn them on when sounds of chanting filtered through the open windows.

"What the hell?" Remy muttered.

Principal Ashcraft strode to the window and muttered a mild curse under her breath. "It's Katherine Edouard and her most rabid PTA moms."

Everyone in the room gathered around the windows to watch as Mrs. Edouard led a small group of women up to the schoolyard, carrying homemade signs proclaiming sex education should be taught at home, not at school.

A van pulled up behind them. A pretty blonde got out carrying a microphone. A cameraman exited the side of the van and followed her toward the marching women.

"Great." Principal Ashcraft turned to Ouida Mae. "As much as the kids need your instruction on sex education, I'm afraid we'll have to postpone Monday's lesson. I'm sure the school board will want to have a say once they see our school plastered all over Louisiana news networks."

Ouida Mae's lips pressed into a thin line. "Understood."

Valentin shook his head. The look on Ouida Mae's face spoke volumes. He could tell that she hated caving into a self-righteous mama.

More than that, she hated that the students wouldn't get the information they needed to make more informed decisions.

Witnessing the dynamics among parents, teachers and administration further drove home the realization that Valentin wasn't ready or mentally equipped to face classrooms full of hormonal teenagers...or worse...their parents.

CHAPTER 5

OUIDA MAE STEWED over the injustice of one squeaky wheel calling the shots for the entire school. As the wife of a local politician, she had other moms who followed her lead like groupies for a rock band, clinging to her shirttails for scraps of attention and limelight.

Refusing to let Katherine Edouard know she'd gotten under her skin, Ouida Mae gathered her belongings and left the building.

As soon as she stepped outside, Katherine and her cronies pointed and yelled, "There she is!"

The pretty blonde reporter hurried toward her. "Miss Maudet, may I have a word with you?"

Valentin inserted himself between the reporter and Ouida Mae. "Do you want to talk to her?" he asked Ouida Mae.

Ouida Mae shook her head.

ELLE JAMES

Valentin and his larger-than-life body remained planted between the reporter and Ouida Mae. "No comment," he said to the blonde.

"But Miss Maudet," the reporter tried to get around Valentin to no avail, "we like to present both sides of an argument."

"No, she doesn't," Ouida Mae whispered loud enough for only Valentin to hear. He steered her toward his truck.

"My car is on the other side of the parking lot," she muttered.

"Do you trust me?" he asked.

She glanced up at him and nodded. She barely knew him, yet she trusted him. She'd never trusted a man on one meeting alone. What was it about him?

"Let's get you out of here first," he said. "Once the news team has gone, we'll circle back and get your car."

Glad to let him run interference, Ouida Mae let him lead the way and help her up into the passenger seat of his pickup.

The blonde and her cameraman followed all the way, badgering Ouida Mae for a statement.

Once inside Valentin's truck with the door closed, she took a deep breath and let it out slowly.

Valentin slid behind the driver's wheel and practically closed the door on the reporter's microphone. He shifted into reverse and backed out of the parking space. "I would've thought you'd want to give your side of the story."

Ouida Mae snorted. "I've seen some of her so-called unbiased reports. She doesn't present both sides. She only presents the most sensational side and blows it out of proportion. Since Katherine is married to a state representative, she'll side with Katherine and her cult followers."

She stared straight forward, avoiding eye contact with the Edouard woman. Once they passed the picket line, she released the breath she'd been holding and slumped back against the seat. "Where to?"

"How about we swing by Sweet Temptations for ice cream." He grinned. "My treat."

"If you think you can't be angry eating ice cream..." her lips twitched, "you're one hundred percent correct. Only I should buy it since you're going out of your way to help me."

"Call it professional courtesy as one teacher to another," he said. "You'd do the same for anyone else in the same situation—but you can buy my ice cream as long as you let me take you to dinner tomorrow night."

Her heart fluttered at the thought of having an intimate dinner with this broad-shouldered, former military sexy hunk. The flutter built swiftly into near panic. She hadn't been on a date since... She thought back. Hell, she couldn't remember.

"I can't go out with you tomorrow night," she said, grasping for a plausible excuse. "It's a school night."

"Sunday?" he asked, a single brow cocked in her direction.

"With Monday being a school day, the night before is considered a school night. I have to work on an alternative lesson plan for Monday since my scheduled plan has been placed on hold."

His brow furrowed. "Okay, we won't go out."

A stab of disappointment hit Ouida Mae square in the chest at his easy acceptance of her lame excuse. She didn't have to work hard to alter her scheduled lessons. He could have fought a little harder. Unless he really didn't care whether or not she went to dinner with him. "It's just as well. I'm sure you need time to build your lesson plans, anyway."

His eyebrows shot up. "Do PE teachers have lesson plans?"

"Miss Sutton always had a plan for her students in her PE and her Gifted and Talented classes. I'm sure you can use whatever she had until you design your own."

"That settles it. I'll be at your house tomorrow evening with pizza," he announced as he pulled into a parking space in front of Sweet Temptations, Bayou Mambaloa's only ice cream parlor and candy-making shop. "I need one-on-one guidance so I don't fall flat on my face Monday morning."

"Are you afraid some of the students will eat you alive?" she said with a playful smile.

"Hell, yes." He shifted into park. "I have no experience with teens. Exercise, yes. Kids, no."

"You'll be fine," she said, unbuckling her seatbelt. "You just have to keep them busy. They need structure to keep them in line."

He nodded, his brow creased. "Keep them too busy to plot against me. Got it." He dropped down out of the truck, rounded the hood and arrived at her door as she pushed it open.

Valentin held out his hand.

Ouida Mae placed hers in his and let him help her to the ground. If she leaned forward just a little she could end up in his arms. It took every bit of her control to keep from "accidentally" bumping into him.

He kept her elbow and guided her through the door of Sweet Temptations.

"Ouida Mae," Camille Catoire called out. "What brings you here in the middle of the afternoon on poker night? Do you need some candies for the table or a quart of ice cream?"

Ouida Mae shook her head. "No, we're just here to eat some ice cream. I'll do my grocery shopping after I leave here. If you have anything you want me to get for you tonight, let me know."

"I don't need a thing," Camille said. "I'm bringing beer, Shelby's bringing pretzels and potato chips and

Amelie is bringing her fabulous spinach dip. I don't remember what Felina and Gisele are bringing."

"Do I even need to stop at the general store?" Ouida Mae asked with a laugh.

Camille's eyes narrowed and then widened. "Wine. Felina is bringing the wine. I think Gisele is bringing her grandmother's famous cheese ball."

Ouida Mae grimaced. "Is she spiking it with magic?"

"Knowing Gisele, she'll add something questionable." Camille grinned. "Remember the time she infused the cheese ball with a spell that reduced our inhibitions?"

Ouida Mae's cheeks heated. "I'm still trying to live that one down."

Camille chuckled. "I'll never forget seeing you run down Main Street wearing nothing but one of Gisele's see-through caftans and singing at the top of your lungs "I'm so pretty.""

The whole time Camille was recounting the story, Ouida Mae was slicing her hand across her throat. But Camille was not to be dissuaded from sharing the story in front of the man Ouida Mae had just met.

A wicked smile curled his lips. "Is there a naughty side to the junior high science teacher?"

"Absolutely," Camille said. "Freed from her inhibitions, she's a wild child." Camille turned her attention to Valentin and held out her hand. "Camille Catoire at your service. Do I know you? I've seen you around town."

"Valentin Vachon." Valentin took her hand in his. "I blew into town with Remy Montage's crew of Brotherhood Protectors. However, I will be filling in as the PE teacher at the junior high until Miss Sutton returns."

Camille's brow furrowed. "You are a brave man. Some of the stories Ouida Mae tells make my toes curl. I don't think I could do it. Teenagers are scary beasts. I get them in here all the time." Her grin returned. "No, really, some of them are great. And some of them are just mischievous, working the orneriness out of their systems—like some of us when we were their ages."

"Their bodies are going through so many changes. They're just trying to figure out what to do with all that energy and change," Ouida Mae said. "I like working with young teens. They're bright, intelligent and soaking in everything around them."

Camille sighed. "That's our Ouida Mae. Ever the optimist." She clapped her hands together and lifted an ice cream scoop. "Okay, my sweets, what tempts your tastebuds today?"

Ouida Mae shook her head. "I might be the optimist, but you're the sweetest and so creative when it comes to candies and ice cream. You know my favorites. I'll take my usual two scoops."

"One scoop of Rocky Road and one scoop of Very,

Berry Strawberry coming right up." Camille dipped the scoop into the Rocky Road first and rolled it around, making the ice cream ball bigger before fitting it into a waffle cone. Then she repeated the process in the strawberry adding that scoop to the top of the Rocky Road. She handed the sweet treat to Ouida Mae. "Just the way you like it."

"Perfect." Ouida Mae licked some of the chocolate that dripped onto her hand

"And for you?" Camille dipped her scoop into the water and waited for Valentin's selection.

"Actually, as good as the chocolate and strawberry look, I'm a pralines and cream fan. Two scoops, please."

"A man who knows what he likes and isn't afraid to ask," Camille said with a wink. Seconds later, she handed him a waffle cone with two scoops of pralines and cream.

Ouida Mae fumbled in her purse for her wallet.

Camille held up a hand. "On the house."

"You can't make a living giving away your ice cream," Ouida Mae said.

"I heard what happened at the junior high yesterday afternoon. I would've closed the shop and come to help clean up, but I had several orders of pralines and chocolate I had to produce for my distributor in New Orleans. I'm sorry I wasn't there to help." Camille came out from behind the counter and hugged Ouida Mae.

"He didn't attack me," Ouida Mae assured her.

"But he attacked poor Mr. Jones, and he could've attacked you had you been in your room at the time."

"I'm really sad about Mr. Jones. It makes me so angry that somebody would hurt such a gentle soul," Ouida Mae said. "I hope the sheriff finds the bastard soon."

"Me, too," Camille hugged her once more and then stepped away. "I worry about you living out there on the edge of the Bayou all by yourself. What if he gets more personal and targets your home? I'd hate for anything to happen to our poker night optimist."

Ouida Mae frowned. "Do you think he'll attack my house? Maybe we should call off the poker game tonight. I don't want any of my friends hurt."

"Anyone who would attack your house filled with six strong, independent women would have to be out of his mind. Besides, we can keep an eye on you with us there." Camille crossed her arms over her chest. "We can't cancel poker night. It's tradition."

Ouida Mae loved Camille's unwavering support, but she still worried about her friends. "Will the others feel the same?"

"We'll have an officer of the law amongst us. Shelby always brings her gun. And we've all been through self-defense training." Camille lifted a confident chin. "We're covered."

"You know," Valentin started, "if you need

someone to lurk in the shadows around your place, I'm available."

"That's nice of you to offer," Ouida Mae said, "but you have plans with your guys at the Crawdad Hole."

"They wouldn't miss me."

Camille held up a hand. "No way. It's girls' night."

"Message received," Valentin said. "Thank you for the ice cream."

"You're welcome." Camille frowned. "I'm counting on you to keep an eye on my girl at the school and anywhere else you two might be together." She waved her hand between Ouida Mae and Valentin. "I'm getting a more than friends vibe here if I'm not mistaken."

"No, no." Ouida Mae was quick to set her friend straight. "We just met today."

"It only takes a moment to click with the right person," Camille said with a knowing smile.

"Says one with experience?" Ouida Mae challenged.

Camille's smile faded. "Yeah. Trust me when I say don't waste a moment of time together with someone you love. You might only have that moment together."

Ouida Mae sensed her friend had been holding back something she should know. Had Camille loved and lost someone Ouida Mae didn't know about? She'd make the time to find out very soon.

Valentin and Ouida Mae left Sweet Temptations

and strolled down Main Street to a park with a picnic table, where they ate their ice cream and people-watched.

Ouida Mae knew all the permanent residents in Bayou Mambaloa and loved pointing them out and sharing their quirks and good qualities with Valentin.

"You love this town, don't you?" he commented.

She nodded. "I do. I come from a long line of Maudets who've lived here for a couple of centuries." She ate the tip of the cone and wiped her fingers on the napkin. "My parents took me on trips all over the country and parts of the world. But I always liked coming home to Bayou Mambaloa. My friends are my people."

"And they want you to be safe." He held out his hand. "May I see your cell phone?"

Her brow wrinkled as she extracted her cell phone from her purse and handed it to him. "Why do you need my phone?"

"Open it, please."

She did and watched as he added a number to her contact list and then his name. "Now, I'm just a phone call away," he said and handed her phone back to her. "You can call me anytime, day or night, or not at all if that suits you. I just want you to know I'll be there if you need me."

Her heart melted at his gesture. "Thanks." She placed a call to his number.

When his phone rang, he answered and smiled at her. "See? I'll answer anytime you call."

"And now you have my number," she said. "If you need anything, directions to the closest strawberry farm, notes about members of our community or the best place on the bayou for rare bird sightings, I can help you."

Ouida Mae took her offer a step further, channeling Gisele's cheeseball loaded with a spell to reduce her inhibitions and added, "Or if you just want a friend to talk to, I'll answer, day or night... as long as it's not during school or our girls' poker game," she said with a grin.

He stared down at his cell phone and then back up at her. "Thank you. That means a lot to me, knowing I have a friend I can call."

Ouida Mae laughed. "You have at least a dozen you came with to Bayou Mambaloa."

He nodded. "Any one of them would take a bullet for me, and I would do the same for them, but I wouldn't call them to just shoot the breeze."

"Well, you can call me. Living alone gets... lonely sometimes. I'd shoot the breeze with you." She glanced down at her phone. "Dang. I have company coming to my house in a couple of hours, and I still haven't gone for groceries. I'll need you to drop me at the school to get my car before I go to Broussard's."

"The store is on the way to the school. Let me

help you shop. I'm good at pushing a cart and carrying dozens of bags in one trip."

She looked at the man, wondering if he was real. "Seriously? I've never met a man who *likes* to shop."

He shrugged. "It's not the shopping," he said. "It's the company."

"Okay then. You can push the cart. But I draw the line at squeezing fruit. That's my job."

"Deal." He rose, extended a hand to Ouida Mae and helped her to her feet.

That spark of electricity zinged through her body at his touch and made her heart flutter erratically.

He didn't release her hand after helping her stand. Instead, he held it in his as they walked back to his truck.

It was like they were a couple happily strolling along Main Street without a care in the world and it didn't matter who saw them.

Ouida Mae was known to most of the full-time residents. By the time they reached Valentin's truck, the gossipy ones' tongues would be wagging. She'd hear about it at the poker game that night.

Still, she didn't free her hand. Ouida Mae liked the way her small hand fit in Valentin's larger, stronger grip. He made her feel protected and cared for.

Lifting her chin, Ouida Mae let a smile spread across her face. Let the old biddies gossip. She didn't give a darn what they'd say when it felt right and so good.

Valentin drove her to Broussard's. While he pushed the cart, she loaded it with food and drinks her friends weren't bringing, as well as paper napkins. While she checked out with Alan Broussard, Valentin bagged the groceries.

"It must be poker night." Chrissy Broussard emerged from the storeroom behind the counter, carrying a baby on her hip.

"Hey, Chrissy. That's right," Ouida Mae said. "You know you're welcome to join us anytime."

Chrissy shifted the baby to the other hip. "I'd love to, but five children are a lot to manage alone while helping out with the store." She smiled at the baby on her hip. "Maybe when all five of you little terrorists are in school, I'll have a chance to join the big girls."

"I'll watch the kids if you'd like to join them tonight," her husband offered.

Chrissy gave her husband a twisted smile. "The other part of that equation is that by the end of the day, I'm too exhausted to think." She patted her husband's arm. "But I'll take a rain check."

"Anytime, darlin'. You're amazing." He kissed her cheek. "You know I love you."

Chrissy laughed. "Oh, I know how much you love me. I have five children to show for it."

"I don't know how you keep up with five little ones," Ouida Mae said.

"I don't know how you do it," Chrissy said. "Dealing with dozens of teenagers has to be a lot harder. You must have the patience of the saint." She shifted her gaze to Valentin. "Is this your new man everyone's talking about?"

Not even thirty minutes after holding Valentin's hand on Main Street, the gossip had already made it to Broussard's.

Ouida Mae's cheeks heated. "He's not my new man. He's the new PE teacher at the junior high. You know Valentin, don't you?"

"Of course we do," Chrissy replied. "He's with Remy's bunch of Brotherhood Protectors."

Alan chuckled. "Was saving the world so boring you decided dealing with teens would be more fun?"

"Something like that," Valentin said with a wry grin. "After Ouida Mae's classroom was trashed, and Mr. Jones was hurt, the regular PE teacher decided she needed a sabbatical. I offered to help. Landry is filling in for the janitor until the principal can find a replacement."

"Well, we appreciate your team jumping in to help the community." Chrissy nodded toward Ouida Mae. "Stay safe, my friend. I need you to stick around long enough for me to be able to join you at the poker game." She winked. "Have fun for me tonight."

"We will," Ouida Mae said and grabbed a bag of groceries.

Valentin grabbed the rest.

Together, they carried them out to the truck and laid them on the backseat.

Valentin drove them to the junior high where Ouida Mae's car was parked. When she started to take the groceries out of the backseat, Valentin shook his head.

"Leave them," he said. "I'll follow you to your house and help you unload and get ready for poker night."

"You don't have to do that," Ouida Mae said. "It won't take me a second to transfer the groceries to my car."

"I know you're a strong, independent woman and don't need my help, but I'd really like to do this for you." He gave her a pleading puppy dog face that melted her knees and her lady parts.

She couldn't resist. "OK then, you can follow me."

As she drove to her house, she glanced at her rearview mirror several times and almost missed her turn. The thought of Valentin entering her house with his broad shoulders, taking up all the space, had her insides quivering. If her friends weren't scheduled to show up in less than an hour, she could think of a few things she'd rather do with the new PE teacher.

Not that he was her boyfriend, nor was he her lover.

Yet, the little devil on her shoulder whispered in her ear.

Don't be ridiculous, she told herself.

What would a former military guy see in a boring junior high science teacher? He could have any woman he chose to grace with just one of his smiles.

Still, he was following her out to her house with an offer to help her set up for poker night. He'd held her hand walking down Main Street. They'd had ice cream together.

What did it mean?

As she exited her car, her heart sputtered, and her pulse raced. She'd be alone in her house with this man. Her thoughts sped ahead. Had she left the house a mess? Had she made her bed? Were there dishes in the sink?

Then she reminded herself that she never left her house a mess, always made her bed and did her dishes as soon as she was finished with them.

Having a man over had completely rattled her.

No.

Having Valentin over had her rattled.

She shifted into park, got out of her car and hurried over to help gather groceries.

"I've got these," Valentin said, "if you can unlock the door." He had several bags looped over each arm.

"Good grief," Ouida Mae said. "You can't do everything."

"Watch me," he said with a wink.

That would be a challenge with him behind her. Ouida Mae hurried up the steps to her little cottage and quickly unlocked the door. She held it open while Valentin carried all the bags inside.

"The kitchen is straight through to the back and hang a right," she said and followed him down a short hallway, enjoying the view of his bulging biceps, trim hips and thick thighs.

The hallway was entirely too short.

He set the bags on the counter. With Valentin emptying the bags and Ouida Mae stowing the items, it didn't take long to put everything where it needed to be.

"What else do you need a hand with?" he asked.

She smiled. "I can manage the rest on my own," she said. "I just have to chop some veggies, make up a charcuterie board, add a leaf to the table and sweep the floor."

"While you chop veggies, I'll sweep and add the leaf to the table," Valentin said. "Your ladies will be here soon. The least I can do is help with the grunt work."

Ouida Mae frowned. "Are you sure you don't have better things to do?"

He shook his head. "My guys aren't meeting at the Crawdad Hole for another hour. Won't take me more than fifteen minutes to shower and change."

Ouida Mae's eyes widened. "I almost forgot." She glanced down at her old jeans and T-shirt with French gray splattered across the front. "I need to shower and change." She glanced at the clock. "Shoot. That doesn't leave me much time."

"Then go. I'll do the sweeping, extend the table and wash the vegetables."

When she hesitated, he waved a hand. "Go. The clock's ticking. Where's the broom?"

"In the mud room," Ouida Mae called over her shoulder as she headed for her bedroom. Once she'd shut the door, she pulled her T-shirt over her head, kicked off her shoes and shucked her jeans. She was about to drop her thong panties and unclip her bra when she remembered that the little cottage had only one bathroom. And it was in the hall with her bathrobe hanging on the back of the door.

Living alone, she usually left her bedroom door open and strode naked across the hall to the bathroom.

She'd never even thought about it.

Until she had a man in the kitchen at the end of the hallway.

Not wanting to put on her dirty clothes, she gathered a clean blouse, jeans and underwear. It would only take a second to cross the hall. If she timed it right, she could cross without flashing the PE teacher. And really, what would he see he wouldn't see on a beach?

Women wore thong bikinis all the time.

Just not this woman. Not in public.

She eased open her door and peered down the hall.

Valentin swept past the opening at the end of the hall and disappeared.

Ouida Mae yanked open the door and dashed barefoot across the hall. When she reached the bathroom, she fumbled with the old door handle. In the process of twisting it, she dropped her jeans and panties.

One second turned into two as she bent to retrieve the fallen items.

"Ouida Mae, where is the table leaf—"

Ouida Mae jerked to attention, clutching her jeans to her chest, her eyes wide as she stared at Valentin standing in the hallway. For a moment, he stood transfixed. Then he visibly swallowed and said, "Sorry." He turned his back, murmuring something that sounded suspiciously like *not sorry.*

Ouida Mae's cheeks burned, but she felt more like giggling at the situation. "If you pull the tabletop apart, you'll find the leaf stored inside."

As she stood almost naked in the hallway, staring at Valentin's back, the heat in her cheeks spread down her torso to the juncture of her thighs.

She needed a shower.

He needed a shower.

Her mouth opened to invite him to join her.

A soft knock sounded on the front door.

Ouida Mae spun, still holding her clothes in front of her.

The door opened, and a female voice called out, "Ouida Mae, help has arrived." Gisele pushed through the door, followed by Shelby and Felina Faivre, who owned the flower shop.

They were halfway down the hallway when Gisele came to an abrupt stop. "Oh. Sorry, did we come too soon? You haven't even had a chance to shower."

"We just thought you could use some help—" Shelby's gaze shot past Ouida Mae. "Oh, wait. You already have help." She waved a hand. "Hey, Valentin."

Ouida Mae glanced over her shoulder to where Valentin stood several feet closer to her and facing her nearly naked, thong-covered bottom. That heat at her core flamed up into her cheeks.

"Ladies," Felina whispered loud enough for Ouida Mae to hear, "maybe we should leave and give them some privacy."

"That won't be necessary," Valentin said. "I was about to leave after I finished one last thing." He disappeared into the kitchen.

"And I was about to jump in the shower," Ouida Mae choked out.

"Uh-huh." Gisele winked. "Was Val's one last thing to join you before our untimely appearance?"

"Of course not," Ouida Mae answered, her cheeks still flaming. She was a terrible liar. Her face gave her away every time. She'd thought about inviting Valentin to shower with her but hadn't actually asked. So, it wasn't really a lie.

Valentin reappeared. "The table is all set up. I'd better get going. The guys will be expecting me soon."

He took a few long strides toward Ouida Mae. As he passed her, his hand brushed her bare arm. "See you on Monday," he murmured. Then he grinned at the others. "Enjoy poker night, ladies."

All gazes followed the man out the front door.

As soon as he disappeared, the three ladies faced Ouida Mae.

"Oh, sweetie," Gisele said with a sly smirk, "tell us all."

"Nothing to say," Ouida Mae squeaked, backing into the bathroom. "I'll be out after my shower." She slammed the door shut to the sound of her so-called friends' laughter.

Holy moly, she'd come so close to asking a man, a near stranger, to join her in the shower.

Had her friends not come when they had, Ouida Mae could have been lathering Valentin's broad chest and other parts further south.

She should feel relief that her friends had come at that exact moment and saved her from potential embarrassment.

But all she felt was regret and an itch that remained completely unscratched.

CHAPTER 6

WOW. Just wow.

As Valentin drove away. His body still hummed, and his blood burned with desire.

When he'd stepped into the hallway to find Ouida Mae standing there in nothing but a bra and thong panties, the air had been sucked right out of his lungs, leaving him speechless.

Her mouth and the twinkle in her eyes had punched him square in the chest when she'd scraped paint from his hair. But that perfectly rounded ass in those thong panties...

As a man who could never commit, he was at risk of falling for this cute little science teacher.

Hard.

Not just because of a scrap of material disappearing between her butt cheeks or her plump lips begging to be kissed. She was smart and funny, and she cared about her students and community.

He could actually picture himself forty years older, sitting in a rocking chair on the front porch of her cute little cottage. He'd be holding her hand and reminiscing about that time he caught her in her hallway in nothing but a bra and panties. They'd laugh about the looks on their friends' faces.

He'd continue to hold her hand, rocking slowly in the sultry bayou air. Eventually, they'd get up and go to their bedroom, make old-people sex, slow and perfect, and fall asleep in each other's arms.

He'd never imagined anything like that before now. A week ago, that kind of image would've grossed him out. But not now. Knowing Ouida Mae with her heart, her spunk and her ability to make the most out of situations had changed his perspective entirely.

Had settling down in a small town brought him to this moment? Was he getting soft?

The tightness in his groin begged to differ.

Yes, she turned him on, but he liked her company even when it was non-sexual. He'd enjoyed grocery shopping with her. Eating ice cream had been a treat —because of her.

Valentin headed back to the boarding house where he was still living, not having found his own place yet. He showered and changed into clean jeans and a button-down blue chambray shirt. As he stepped out into the hallway, he ran into Landry.

"Hey, Val, you clean up well." Landry looked him over. "You even got all the paint out of your hair. Do you want to ride together to the Crawdad Hole? The others left half an hour ago."

"Why didn't you ride with them?" Valentin asked as they fell in step together, heading for the exit.

"I went for a run and didn't get back in time to shower before they left." He looked at Valentin with narrowed eyes. "Where have you been? We were done at the school hours ago."

"Since we spent so much of the day getting her classroom back in order," Valentin said, "I helped Miss Maudet get her house ready for her girls' poker night."

Landry snorted. "I'm surprised she let you in her house. They seem to fiercely guard the girls-only aspect of poker night."

"Yes, they do." Valentin's lips curved in a sardonic grin. "I left there as some of the ladies were arriving."

"I take it you're treating this assignment as more than just filling in as a PE teacher," Landry said. "Do you think whoever trashed her classroom will come after her next?"

"The thought has crossed my mind," Valentin said. "If you want to ride with me, I'd gladly take you to the bar. But you'll need to catch a ride with one of the others back to the boarding house. I might swing by Miss Maudet's place later to check on her."

Landon's eyebrows rose. "And interrupt the poker game?"

Valentin chuckled. "No, I'll wait until after the game is over and the ladies have dispersed."

"Fair enough," Landry said. "I'm sure I can catch a ride with someone else. But we better get there before they consume all the good food. Tonight's crawfish boil night. I don't want to miss out on that."

The two men climbed into Valentin's truck and drove to the Crawdad Hole just outside Bayou Mambaloa. The parking lot was full, and music thrummed through the walls of the building.

They found the rest of their crew inside, gathered around a long table, digging into a huge spread of food. The center of the table was covered with a plastic sheet and piled high with crawfish, corn and potatoes. Each man had a plastic bib tied around his neck and a large mug of beer at his elbow.

"About time you showed up." Remy broke open the shell of a crawdad and sucked the meat out of it.

"Pull up a seat, and dive in," Beau said.

Valentin and Landry dragged chairs up to the table. The other men scooted around to allow them in.

Danny French, the petite red-haired waitress, appeared, handed them plastic bibs and a wad of napkins and took their orders for drinks. For the next twenty minutes, Valentin filled up on the Cajun spiced mud bugs, corn, and potatoes, washing them down with beer.

When they'd gone through all of the food on the table, the team sat back in their seats, wiping their hands on napkins and towelettes.

"Damn, that was good," Gerard said, patting his belly. "It's a good thing they only do this once a month, or I'd be as big as a barn."

"You *are* as big as a barn, Gerard," Lucas said.

Gerard raised both eyebrows. "Jealous?"

"Not at all." Lucas raised his empty mug.

The waitress appeared and swapped the empty mug with a full one.

"Did Shelby get a match on any of the fingerprints they lifted from Ouida Mae's classroom?" Valentin asked Remy.

Remy shook his head. "No. And Mr. Jones is still in a coma. I don't know that Jones would've recognized him anyway. From what Miss Maudet said, the intruder wore a ski mask."

As they talked, Danny cleaned up the crawfish shells and empty corn cobs from the center of the table, pulling the plastic sheet all onto a large platter. "I'll be right back with a damp rag."

"What did you think about Kathryn Edouard's line of protesters showing up on the tail end of the cleanup effort?" Remy asked.

"I think she's one determined woman," Valentin

said, "and that she's burying her head in the sand. Anyone who doesn't believe teenagers are already thinking about sex, if not already doing it, needs a wake-up call."

"If you ask me, they're all thinking about it and most of them doing it." Danny, the waitress, leaned between Remy and Lucas to swipe a clean rag across the table. "Especially the popular boys, like Katherine's son, Chase."

"Shelby says Katherine's husband is Harvey Edouard, an attorney running for governor of Louisiana."

"That's right. He's been campaigning for the better part of a year. He slowed down when he ran out of money, which must've made Katherine unhappy. She had to give up her twice-a-day coffee runs for a few weeks."

The waitress moved to the end of the table in front of Landry and Valentin and continued cleaning the table.

Landry and Valentin held their beer mugs out of the way.

"Seems her husband is back on track," Danny said. "Must have found some more funding for his campaign. Their son, Chase, is the quarterback on the junior high football team. Katherine's thrown herself into being the pillar of righteousness for the community—whether we want her to be or not."

"Do you think she might be behind the attack?" Valentin asked.

Danny straightened with the cloth in her hand. "Katherine?" Her brow furrowed. "I doubt it seriously. Her husband is a district attorney. He puts criminals away. Before Katherine married Harvey, she worked as a corporate attorney in New Orleans. She's smart, if a little overzealous, in her attempt to shape this community into her version of perfect. Katherine's super conscious of hers and her husband's reputation, so she wouldn't risk it by hiring someone to trash a public school."

"Danny," Remy called out from the other end of the table, "you know a lot of people. Is there anyone else who would be offended by Miss Maudet teaching sex ed and natural sciences in her classroom?"

Danny snorted. "It's always easy to point to the most notorious family in Bayou Mambaloa," she said.

Remy nodded. "The Fontenots?"

"I didn't say it, but if the price is right, any one of them would shoot your mother if that's what you paid them to do." She ran her cloth over the length of the table and straightened. "Is there anything else I can get you, gentlemen?"

"I'll take another beer," Landry said.

Danny's eyes narrowed. "You drivin'?"

"No," Remy answered for Landry. "I am. Could

you bring me some hot coffee? Black, no milk or sugar."

"I'll have the same," Valentin added.

"You got it." Danny took orders from the others and hurried away.

"Other than the Edouard woman, who would have motivation to trash Miz Mo's classroom?" Valentin asked.

Remy tipped his head. "It might not hurt to check into the Fontenots. See if they're up to no good."

Loud voices at the entrance of the bar drew their attention to three men who had just arrived.

"Speak of the devils," Lucas said. "Aren't those three men members of the Fontenot family?"

Remy turned towards the door, and his lips pressed into a tight line. "I recognize the two older men as Dan and Ray Fontenot, and I've seen the younger one with them occasionally."

Danny returned with two coffees and another round of beer for those who weren't driving. "That's Regis, Dan's nephew. He's been in and out of trouble all his life. Dan and Ray, the only two men besides Pierre Fontenot worth two hoots, are trying to bring him under their wings and make a decent human out of him."

"Are they having any luck?" Valentin asked.

At that moment, Regis shoved another man who happened to get out of his chair as the three men passed by.

The man he'd shoved spun unsteadily and lifted his fists. "No need to be rude."

"Then don't get in my way," Regis's voice carried through the room.

Before either man could take a swing at the other, Dan and Ray each grabbed one of Regis's arms and hustled him to a far corner of the room.

Danny chuckled. "I think Regis needs more work. He's still too full of himself."

"Would be nice to know where he was yesterday afternoon around the time Miss Maudet's classroom was trashed," Remy said.

"I'll see what I can find out," Danny said.

"Don't do it if it will put you in danger," Landry said.

She snorted. "Honey, I'm a waitress in a bar. I can handle just about anything." She walked away with a tray balanced over her head.

"She's feisty," Landry said. "I like her."

"You and every red-blooded male in here," Simon Sevier muttered.

Lucas laughed. "And half the females. Danny's a pistol."

"Just don't piss her off," Gerard said. "I've seen her throw down a three-hundred-pound redneck for pinching her ass."

Landry chuckled. "I'd have paid good money to see that."

ELLE JAMES

"Stick around," Gerard said, "that Regis boy is about to have a come-to-Jesus-meeting with Danny."

All gazes went to Danny French's diminutive form as she pulled Regis Fontenot's thumb back so far he almost tipped out of his chair.

"The woman has some skills," Landry said.

Valentin wondered if she'd taken the same self-defense class as Ouida Mae.

He glanced down at his watch. The poker game was probably in full swing. Hanging around the Crawdad Hole for another hour seemed like forever.

Simon leaned toward Valentin. "Got a hot date?"

Before Valentin could answer, Beau spoke, "Moving in fast on Miz Mo?"

All his teammates' attention shifted to Valentin.

"That's right..." Lucas turned away from Danny and Regis. "You two only had eyes for each other while we were fixing up her classroom today. Something going on between you and the sexy science teacher?"

Nothing his teammates needed to know about.

"No," Valentin said. "I'm just keeping an eye on her in case the attacker decides to go after her next."

"Glad to see you taking the assignment more seriously than as just a PE teacher," Remy said. "I hear you took her to Sweet Temptations for ice cream and were seen walking hand-in-hand down Main Street afterward."

Valentin's lips twisted into a smile. "It's good to know the grapevine travels fast in Bayou Mambaloa."

Remy grinned. "I also got word from Shelby that you were at Ouida Mae's place when some of the ladies arrived for the poker game." The man's grin became a wide smile.

Don't go there, Valentin thought. "Yeah, so?"

Remy went there. "Apparently, Ouida Mae was in an awkward position."

"Damn, Valentin. Moving in fast, are you?" Beau clapped a hand on Valentin's shoulder.

"What position was that?" Lucas asked.

"Enquiring minds want to know," Simon said. "Missionary, doggy-style, up against the wall—"

"Guys," Valentin interrupted, "give the lady a little respect. Nothing happened."

Although he wished something had.

The image of her in that thong played over and over in his mind like a reel on continuous replay.

"Man, you can't leave us hanging like that," Beau said. "Tell All."

"Nothing happened," Valentin insisted, tired of their teasing and ready to head toward Ouida Mae's place, even if it was too early.

"Guys, Valentin is a gentleman." Remy held up his hands. "And gentlemen don't kiss and tell." He spoiled his stern talk with a wicked grin.

"Not helping," Valentin said. "And there was no kissing to talk about." He pushed his feet and tossed some money on the table. "I'm calling it a night. Enjoy the rest of your evening."

"Going to see if they'll make an exception for you at the poker game?" Simon asked.

"No." Valentin gave a half-wave, turned and left the building.

Once outside, he stood for a moment, drew in a deep breath of fresh air and let it out slowly.

The door opened and closed behind him. A moment later, Remy joined him.

"Shelby just texted me. She's on her way home to get some rest. The pregnancy makes her tired sooner. I'm headed home myself." He stood for a moment longer. "She also said the poker game broke up early, in case you're thinking of swinging by to check on Miz Mo before calling it a night."

There was no teasing in Remy's tone. Valentin appreciated that. Ouida Mae was his assignment, and Remy knew Valentin would take it seriously.

"Good to know," Valentin said. "Have a good evening." He headed for his truck, climbed in and drove out of the parking lot and back toward the little cottage on the edge of the bayou, possibly with a little more anticipation than he should have felt for "just" an assignment.

Ouida Mae didn't know that his job as a PE teacher was more than just wrangling teens. He was there to make sure Ouida Mae and the students in her class were safe from the attacker in case he returned.

If he showed up on her doorstep, he could make the excuse that he thought she might need a little help cleaning up after the poker party. Or he could say that he wanted to make sure she was okay after the disturbing attack on her classroom.

Or he could say that he was attracted to her and wanted to see if she felt the same.

No. It was too soon. She was a woman in a vulnerable position. He didn't want to come on too strong, too fast, and scare her away or have her cling to him because she was scared more so than she cared.

Valentin decided to do a drive-by rather than stop and knock on her door. He wasn't entirely sure he could keep his hands to himself this late at night and with that woman.

But he couldn't feel right about going back to his place without at least checking one more time on the science teacher.

CHAPTER 7

SOME OF THE ladies stayed to help clean up after the poker game. Ouida Mae would've preferred that they leave and let her do it herself. She had a lot on her mind and had been less than focused on the game. And she wasn't the only one.

The game hadn't even begun when the teasing started. Ouida Mae's cheeks still flamed every time she thought about standing in the hallway in next to nothing when her friends had come through the front door and spied Valentin behind her. She had hurried to explain herself, but friends had just given her knowing looks and quickly filled in the others as they arrived.

Which made for an uncomfortable evening, playing poker with the girls. She wished she had canceled the game when she'd had the chance.

And if she had canceled the game, she might've had that shower with the sexy PE teacher after all.

A shiver of desire slipped across her skin as she loaded the dishwasher with glasses and plates. She'd run the load in the morning after breakfast. For the moment, she wanted to sip a glass of wine, listen to soft music and lie in bed with B.O.B., her battery-operated-boyfriend.

She'd learned long ago that she didn't need a man to satisfy all her needs. That's when she'd gone all the way to New Orleans to an adult toy store and purchased B.O.B.

After all, how many human boyfriends would be content to be shoved in a drawer and brought out, at the most, once a week and only if she felt like it?

Ouida Mae poured her glass of wine, selected her favorite soft rock music on her cell phone and connected it with her mini speaker.

As romantic music filled the air, she rummaged in the bottom drawer of her nightstand for B.O.B.

As her fingers wrapped around the long shaft, she heard something besides the music. She froze and strained her ears to listen to the sound again.

There it was. Maybe footsteps on the porch?

Ouida Mae adjusted the volume lower on her speaker.

The muffled creak of a wood board made Ouida Mae's pulse quicken. She released B.O.B. and grabbed her cell phone, her first thought to dial 911. When she brought up her contacts list, Valentin's name was at the top.

She pressed his number, turned off the light on her nightstand, and tiptoed to her bedroom door. Twisting the lock in the door handle didn't give her much of a sense of relief. Anyone could kick that door in with a little effort. As she waited for Valentin's phone to ring on his end, she slipped into her closet and closed the door. Ouida Mae eased into the back of her closet, sliding the hanging clothes in front of her.

He answered on the second ring, "Ouida Mae, are you OK?"

"I don't know," she whispered. "I heard footsteps on my porch."

"Have all your friends left?" Valentin asked.

"Yes," she said. "Twenty minutes ago."

"Any chance someone forgot something?"

"I didn't find anything when I was cleaning up."

"Where are you now?" he asked.

"I'm hiding in the closet in my bedroom."

"Good," he said. "Did you call 911?"

"No. I called you first. Where are you?" she asked.

"Driving," he answered. "I can be at your place in two minutes if you want me there."

"Yes, please," she answered, speaking so softly she hoped he could hear.

"I'm on my way," he assured her. "Stay on the phone with me."

"I will." There was no way she'd hang up on him. He was like a lifeline to her.

"Are your doors locked?" The warm timbre of his voice helped keep her from freaking out.

"Yes," she said. "I locked them after everyone left. Shelby wouldn't drive away until I did. She personally checked all the window locks while she was here."

"Do you have a weapon?" he asked.

"I don't have a gun," she said, "but I have a signed baseball bat one of my students gave me."

"Is it where you can reach it?"

Ouida Mac felt around in the darkness until she located the bat leaning in a corner of the closet. "Yes, I have it."

"I'm near your driveway now," he said. "Stay where you are until I tell you to come out."

"I'll stay."

"If I don't give you the all-clear in three minutes or less, dial 911."

Ouida Mae shivered. "Okay."

"I have to turn off my phone now, but only long enough to check out the area around your house."

"Be careful," she said.

"Will do." The call ended, leaving Ouida Mae in a dark closet, listening to the soft strains of a love song. She stared at the time on her cell phone and watched as a minute ticked by.

Then another minute passed.

Halfway through the next minute, she poised her fingers over the numbers, prepared to dial 911.

Her phone vibrated in her hand, scaring her so much she fumbled and dropped it onto the floor of her closet. It had vibrated four times by the time she found it recognized Valentin's number displayed. Before she could answer, the vibrations ceased.

A loud knock sounded on her front door.

"Ouida Mae!" Valentin's Voice shouted. "Ouida Mae! Open up. It's me."

Ouida Mae scrambled to her feet, flung the closet doors open and ran for the bedroom door. When she tried to open it, she couldn't. But then she remembered that she'd locked it and twisted the button in the handle. As she ran down the hallway, Valentin called out her name again.

"I'm coming," she cried. When she reached the front door, she disengaged the lock in the handle, twisted the deadbolt and flung the door open.

"Thank God," Valentin said. "I was about to break down your door. I didn't find anything outside your house. I was about to think your intruder had made it inside. Are you OK?"

Ouida Mae nodded and then shook her head, tears welling in her eyes.

"Oh, sweetheart, come here." Valentin opened his arms.

Ouida Mae fell into them.

She stood for a long moment in his embrace, her

cheek pressed against his chest, the rapid beat of her heart matching his. When she finally stopped shaking, she looked up into his eyes. "I'm sorry."

Valentin shook his head. "For what?"

"For overreacting," she said, swiping up the moisture on her face. "You didn't find anything or anyone lurking about?"

"No," he said. "But that doesn't mean someone wasn't here. What else would've sounded like footsteps on your porch besides a person walking on it?"

"I could've been mistaken," she said, not yet willing to step out of his embrace.

"Do you want me to look through your house, just to make sure?"

She nodded. "I would like that very much."

Still, she didn't want to move out of his arms.

He shifted her to one side. Keeping his left arm around her, he stepped through her front door with her at his side. After he closed and locked the door behind them, he turned her to face him and cupped her cheeks in his palms. "Stay here for a moment while I look around."

She nodded.

Valentin pressed a quick kiss to her forehead. "I'll be right back."

True to his word, Valentin was back in a minute. "All clear," he said and held out a hand. Ouida Mae placed her hand in his and let him draw her into his arms again.

She sighed. "Maybe I imagined it."

"I don't care if you imagined it or if you really heard it. In the future, don't hesitate to call me." His arms tightened around her briefly, and then he set her away at arm's length. "Do you want me to stick around?"

She stared up into his eyes and wanted to tell him, *Oh, hell yes*. He'd beat the hell out of B.O.B. The sex toy wasn't flesh and fabulous muscles like Valentin. It could only do so much.

But she was already feeling guilty for having sucked him into her imaginary world of intruders. As much as she would love to have him stay, Ouida Mae shook her head. "No. I'm sure you're tired after working all day. It's getting late." She squared her shoulders and smiled up at him. "I'll be okay."

A frown dented Valentin's forehead. "Are you sure?"

No, she wasn't.

"Yes, I am. Now, go home," she said—*before I change my mind.*

He tipped her chin up and stared down into her eyes. "You can call me anytime, and I mean that." Then he bent and brushed his lips across hers.

Ouida Mae leaned up on her toes and deepened the kiss, opening to him.

Valentin's arms came up around her and crushed her to him as his tongue swept past her teeth and caressed hers. Not in a soft, sentimental way. It was as fierce and needy as Ouida Mae felt.

When breathing became necessary, Valentin lifted his head and took in several ragged breaths.

"I shouldn't have done that," he said. "I'm sorry."

"Are you?" she challenged, her voice breathy.

He hesitated for only a moment before he shook his head. "No, I'm not sorry. But I'm supposed to be —" He stopped as if he thought better about what he was about to say.

"Supposed to be what?" she asked.

"Your coworker," he finally said. "We have to work together. I'm sure they have rules at the school about teachers fraternizing."

"This isn't the military," Ouida Mae said.

"No, but I respect you," he said. "I don't want to sabotage your career."

"Kissing me won't sabotage my career." Ouida Mae shook her head. "Are you afraid it will sabotage yours?"

"No," he said, "but I should go before I do something we'll both regret." He backed away, allowing his arms to fall to his sides. "But seriously, call me day or night if you need anything." He turned and strode to the door.

Ouida Mae opened her mouth to tell him she wanted him to stay. She closed it again, recognizing that the man was running away. Had kissing her scared him for some reason? Had she been too forward in deepening the kiss? Was it too soon?

He paused on the threshold without looking back. "Lock the door behind me."

Then he was gone, and the door closed behind him.

Ouida Mae hurried toward the door, wanting to call him back. When her hand reached the knob, she twisted the lock in the handle and then twisted the deadbolt. She leaned her forehead against the cool wooden panel, drew a deep breath and let it out slowly, willing her heartbeat to slow.

That was the problem; everything was moving too fast. She'd only met the guy less than twenty-four hours ago. What did she expect, a declaration of undying love?

She laughed and walked back to her bedroom, then turned the music to the white noise of a rain shower. The glass of wine held no appeal now. She carried it into her kitchen and was pouring it into her sink when a knock sounded on her back door.

A face appeared in the glass window.

Ouida Mae screamed. The glass bumped into the faucet and shattered into the sink, cutting Ouida Mae's hand.

"Miz Mo," the image said. "It's me, Sophie."

Her heart racing, Ouida Mae stared at the ghostly face in the window.

"It's me, Sophie," the face said, "Please," her voice cracked on a sob. "It's me."

Ouida Mae's body trembled as she walked across the kitchen floor to the back door, remembering to breathe. "Sophie?"

"Yes, Miz Mo," the girl said. "Please let me in."

Ouida Mae twisted the lock in the door handle and then the deadbolt and flung open the door. "Sophie, what are you doing here? It's the middle of the night."

The teenager fell through the door into Ouida Mae's arms. "I didn't know where else to go." Her entire body shook with silent sobs.

Ouida Mae stroked a hand down the girl's back while reaching out to close and lock the door with the other hand.

She held the girl in her arms until her sobs subsided. "What happened, Sophie?"

The teenager stepped back and looked up into Ouida Mae's eyes, hers filling with tears again. "I can't go home." Her gaze fell on Ouida Mae's hand. "Oh my God, you're bleeding."

She looked down at her hand and, for the first time, realized she'd been bleeding all along and had left a trail from the sink to the door with blood on the door handle.

Sophie grabbed her wrist and walked her over to the kitchen sink. "I'm so sorry. This is all my fault." She grabbed several paper towels from the roll beside the stove and pressed them against the cut on Ouida Mae's hand. "Hold that while I clean the glass out of the sink."

"Sophie, I can do this," Ouida Mae said. "You need to tell me what's going on. Why can't you go home? Is someone hurting you there?"

"Not since I left a few weeks ago," she said as she carefully picked shards of glass out of the sink and carried them to the trashcan at the end of the counter.

"What do you mean you left a few weeks ago?" Ouida Mae asked. "Where have you been staying?"

"In a shack on the bayou." The girl had finished cleaning the glass out of the sink and once again took Ouida Mae's hand in hers and removed the paper towels. "Hold your hand under the water for a moment. Do you have any gauze and medical tape?"

"In the bottom drawer to the right of the sink," Ouida Mae said.

Sophie dug through the bottom drawer until she found a box full of gauze pads and a roll of white medical tape. After folding a pad into quarters, she used it to apply pressure as she quickly dressed the wound with another piece of gauze and wrapped the tape around Ouida Mae's hand, securing the dressing in place.

"You might need stitches," Sophie said. "I'm so sorry I frightened you. I didn't mean to, but I didn't know where else to go."

"Well, I'm glad you came to me." Ouida Mae shook her head. "I can't believe you've been staying out in the bayou all alone. And in a shack? What shack?"

Sophie grabbed more paper towels and went to work cleaning up the blood trail from the kitchen sink to the back door. "It's just an old, abandoned shack nobody cares about. It looks so rundown, people ignore it."

Sophie carried the bloody paper towels to the trash bin. "Do you have a mop?"

Ouida Mae stepped into the mudroom, grabbed the mop from where it hung on a hook and came back out.

Sophie took the mop from her. "You can't do that with an injured hand. Let me."

"So, you've been staying in the bayou?" Ouida Mae asked.

As Sophie rinsed the mop in the sink, she nodded. "Until yesterday." The teen squeezed the water out of the mop and placed it on the floor. As she mopped, she talked. "After I left the school yesterday, I went out to the shack. Before I reached it, I saw two men in an airboat checking out the shack. I hid my pirogue beneath some overhanging branches so they wouldn't see me and waited for them to leave."

"And they didn't?"

Sophie shook her head. "I waited and waited. When the airboat finally left, only one man went with it. The other man stayed in the shack. I had nowhere else to go. I rowed further away from the shack and tied off beneath a willow tree. I slept in my boat last night."

"Sophie, why can't you go home?" Ouida Mae asked.

Sophie finished mopping and carried the dirty mop to the sink, where she rinsed it and wrang the water out. She hung the mop back in the mudroom before answering Ouida Mae's question. "I can't go back as long as *he's* there." The girl lifted her chin.

"Who?" Ouida Mae asked, her stomach clenching.

"Him," Sophie responded.

"I thought your mother was divorced," Ouida Mae said.

"That's what she tells everyone. She's never been married. She's had one boyfriend after another living with her ever since I can remember."

"What about your father?" Ouida Mae asked.

Sophie looked away. "I don't know who my father is. My mother never told me. I don't think she knows who my father was. She's always either drunk or strung out on some drugs. I only stayed with her as long as I have because I have no relatives that I know of and nowhere else to go."

Ouida Mae sighed. "I take it she has a boyfriend now, and that's why you don't want to go home?"

Sophie nodded.

Ouida Mae didn't know any easy way to ask, but

she had to. "Has he made unwanted advances toward you?"

Sophie looked away. "I always sleep with a knife under my pillow," she said. "The first time he sneaked into my room...well, I was asleep, and I cut him. My mother yelled at me for hurting him. The second time he tried something, he stole my knife from beneath the pillow, so I poked my thumbs in his eyes. While he was screaming obscenities, I left. I haven't been back since, and my mother hasn't come looking for me."

"And how long ago was that?" Ouida Mae asked.

Sophie shrugged. "Five or six weeks, I've lost count."

"Oh, Sophie, I wish I had known." Ouida Mae shook her head. "How have you survived on your own? You're not old enough to have a job. What do you do for food?"

"I was already on the free lunch plan at school, so I was making do with that. Since there's no running water in the shack, I took showers in the gym after PE."

"Sophie, one meal a day isn't enough to sustain a growing teenage body."

"There are a lot of people in this world who get less food than I do, and they survive," she pointed out. "I had more than just the free lunch. My boyfriend swiped canned goods and boxes of cereal from his folks' pantry so that I would have something to eat on the weekends."

"And your boyfriend's parents didn't offer to take you in?"

Sophie's eyes widened. "No way. They don't even know that he's seeing me. They think he's too young to date. They would never understand.

"Who is your boyfriend?" Ouida Mae asked.

Sophie shook her head. "I'd rather not say. I don't want to get him in trouble. He's the only person who has given a damn about me in a long time."

Ouida Mae thought back to all the students in her classrooms, trying to remember one Sophie spent the most time with. As far as she had been able to tell, Sophie was a loner. She didn't hang out in the hallways talking to friends. She sat alone at lunch. The fact that she had a boyfriend surprised Ouida Mae. They had done a good job of keeping that secret from everybody in the school.

And the teen wasn't ready to share that secret with Ouida Mae.

Sophie had enough problems without her inner science teacher pushing for too many answers.

"You can stay here tonight until we can figure out a better alternative. I'm not sure it's legal for me to harbor one of my students without permission from her legal guardian. I'd like to get some legal advice."

Sophie pressed her lips together in a tight line. "If the shack wasn't still occupied, I'd live there. The last thing I want is to be another statistic in the foster care system. But without a place to live, I need help, and I can't do it all on my own anymore."

"I promise to do what I can to help you," Ouida Mae said. "You're welcome to stay in my guest bedroom until we figure it out. The bed is made, the sheets are clean, and there are fresh towels in the bathroom if you'd like to get a shower first."

Sophie turned and walked toward the back door. She stood staring through the glass into the darkness. "I don't know. Maybe I shouldn't have come here. I don't want to cause problems for you. My problems aren't yours. I just didn't know who else to turn to."

"I'm glad you came to me. I'd hate to think of you, living out in that bayou by yourself with nobody to take care of you."

"I haven't had anybody take care of me in a long time. I learned to take care of myself. But there are other issues at stake, and you're the smartest person I know." She gave a crooked smile. "I figured if anyone could make sense of my life, you could. I just don't want to end up like my mother. I don't think she wanted to be the way she is, but I can't let her poor choices determine my path."

"Honey, you're already smarter than most people your age and a lot of people much older than you." Ouida Mae hooked the teenager's arm. "Come, I'll show you where the bathroom is. While you shower,

I'll heat up some of the leftovers from girls' poker night."

Ouida Mae showed her where the guest bedroom was and then stopped in front of the bathroom. "There's shampoo, conditioner, body wash and towels. Help yourself to anything you need."

Sophie's eyes filled with tears. She flung her arms around Ouida Mae. "Thank you, Miz Mo. You're the best teacher I ever had. I want to study science because of you. You make it interesting and fun. I'll try not to get in your way."

"Don't you worry about that," Ouida Mae said. "It'll be nice having a little company for a change."

"Thank you." Sophie gave her one more hug and then stepped past her into the bathroom and closed the door.

Sophie had arrived with only the clothes on her back. Though Sophie hadn't said anything, Ouida Mae figured the girl had had to abandon whatever belongings she'd left in the shack.

Ouida Mae entered her own bedroom, gathered leggings, T-shirts, underclothes, plus a set of shorty pajamas that would fit Sophie and carried the stack into the hallway. She set the items on the floor outside the bathroom door and then moved into the kitchen.

She pulled containers out of the refrigerator, prepared a plate full of food and popped it in the microwave, ready to warm.

The bathroom door creaked open down the hallway.

Ouida Mae pressed the start button on the microwave. By the time the bell dinged on the microwave, Sophie appeared in the kitchen, wearing leggings and an oversized gray T-shirt with the words *Science like Magic but Real* written in bold letters across the front.

"I like the shirt," Sophie said. "Thanks. I rinsed my clothes in the shower. Once they dry, I'll get your clothes back to you."

"You don't have to," Ouida Mae said. "I have a drawer full of T-shirts I rarely wear. You're welcome to go through them and find ones you like. I also have a drawer full of leggings I don't wear to school. I keep promising myself I'll work out and rarely do. You're welcome to go through that drawer as well and find whatever you need or like."

"I'll pay you for them," Sophie said.

"That won't be necessary." Ouida Mae placed a plateful of food on the table. "I hope you're hungry. I'll never be able to eat all the leftovers by myself."

"You didn't have to do that," Sophie said. "But thank you."

Ouida Mae poured a glass of milk and set it on the table in front of Sophie. She heated a mug of hot water in the microwave, dropped a teabag into it and sat across the table from Sophie so she wouldn't have to eat alone.

The girl ate all the food on the plate and drank the entire glass of milk.

Ouida Mae didn't try to start a conversation while the teenager filled her belly.

When she was done, Sophie carried her plate to the sink, rinsed it, and placed it in the dishwasher along with her glass. She returned to the table and asked, "Are you through with your tea?"

"I am," Ouida Mae said. "But I'll get this. You're welcome to watch TV in the living room if you'd like. It's been a busy day for me. I'm headed to bed." She rose from the table and carried her teacup to the sink. "One thing I'd like to ask…" she said before Sophie left the kitchen.

"Yes, ma'am?" Sophie waited for Ouida Mae's question.

"Before you came to my back door, were you here a few minutes earlier, walking across my porch?"

Sophie's brow wrinkled. "No, ma'am. I'd just rode my pirogue up to the dock next door. As I walked up to your house, I saw taillights headed away along your driveway. At first, I thought it was you leaving. But then I saw the light in the kitchen window. That's why I came to that door." She raised her eyebrows. "Why do you ask?

"I thought I heard footsteps on my porch a little earlier. I could be mistaken," she said as she placed the teacup in the dishwasher and followed Sophie out of the kitchen and down the hallway. Sophie went into the guest bedroom while Ouida Mae entered her bedroom.

She stripped out of her jeans, shirt and bra and pulled on her favorite soft jersey pajama shorts and top before sliding between her sheets. She plugged her cell phone into the charger and debated calling Valentin to tell him about the latest development at her home.

When she realized it was well past midnight, she discarded that idea.

Though Valentin had said he would answer the phone day or night, Ouida Mae assumed that meant only if it was an emergency. She would have loved to talk with him, to ask his advice, but she'd wait until a more reasonable hour.

The incidents of the past two days took their toll on Ouida Mae. She laid her head on the pillow with a million thoughts roiling through her head, thinking sleep would be a long time coming. Within seconds, she was out.

Perhaps it was knowing there was another person in the house that made her feel less jumpy. Or she was just that tired. Either way, she slept through the night, waking the next morning to what sounded like someone retching.

Ouida Mae threw back her covers and hurried to locate the sound. It was coming from the bathroom. The door to Sophie's room was open, and Sophie wasn't in her bed.

More sounds of someone throwing up came from the bathroom.

Ouida Mae knocked softly on the door. "Sophie, are you OK?"

"Yes," came her strangled response. "Go away, please."

Unable to leave the teenager while she was in distress, Ouida Mae pushed the door open to find Sophie on her knees in front of the toilet.

"Please, I'm okay," Sophie said and immediately threw up again. She appeared to have purged everything she'd eaten in the night before.

Ouida Mae grabbed a washcloth from the cabinet, soaked it beneath the faucet and wrung it out as best she could with one hand. "Here, take this." She passed the washcloth to Sophie.

The girl pressed it to her face but remained kneeling on the floor.

Ouida Mae found an elastic ponytail holder and gathered Sophie's long dark hair up in one hand. She secured it to the crown of the girl's head in a ponytail and then wrapped the length around it in a loose bun. "Better?"

Sophie nodded. "Thank you."

"Do you think it was something you ate?" Ouida Mae asked.

"I don't think so." Sophie pulled herself upright, closed the toilet and then sat, pressing the damp cloth to her cheeks. "I've been throwing up every morning for the past week, whether I have any food in my stomach or not."

"Have you had a fever?"

Sophie shook her head.

"Any other symptoms? A rash, stomach discomfort, loose bowels?" Ouida Mae asked.

Again, Sophie shook her head. "No. Funny thing is that after I throw up in the morning, I feel fine for the rest of the day. It's just in the morning."

Nausea in the morning only.

Ouida Mae's belly clenched.

"Sophie, when was your last period?" she asked softly.

Sophie lowered the washcloth and met Ouida Mae's gaze. "About the time I left my mother's house. I only remember because I haven't needed any feminine products since living in the shack." The girl's eyes widened. "You don't think—"

Oh, Ouida Mae *did* think.

"Did your mother's boyfriend force himself on you?" Ouida Mae asked, anger rising up her chest and spreading heat into her cheeks.

Sophie shook her head. "No, ma'am. I wouldn't let him." She buried her face in the damp cloth. "Miz Mo, we didn't know... We didn't think it could happen... I thought I ate something bad..." Her words ran together with her sobs.

Ouida Mae knelt on the floor in front of Sophie and gripped the teen's shoulders. "Sophie."

She waited for the girl to look up and meet her gaze. Tears streamed down her cheeks.

"Sophie, honey," Ouida Mae said softly. "No judgment here. Do you understand?"

Sophie nodded.

Ouida Mae drew in a breath, let it out slowly and then asked. "Have you and your boyfriend been... intimate?"

The teenager sobbed, "Y-yes."

Ouida Mae swallowed hard and kept calm when she wanted to say, *Holy Shit.*

CHAPTER 8

AFTER TOSSING and turning through the night, Valentin left his bed in the pre-dawn hours of the morning to go for a run. He carried his cell phone in a band on his arm just in case Ouida Mae called.

He'd reached for his phone several times during the night, checking for any missed texts or calls. Each time, he'd wanted to call to check on the petite science teacher.

On his run that morning, he went further than his normal distance so that he could swing by Ouida Mae's, hoping he'd catch sight of her. Maybe she'd come out on her porch for a cup of coffee in the early hours before it got hot and more humid.

Her car was there, but she didn't appear on the porch.

Valentin almost jogged down to her cottage to

check that everything was all right, but he didn't want to spook her.

Okay, so he did jog halfway down the drive.

A light glowed from one of the windows on the front of the house.

He glanced at his watch.

Ouida Mae was up early.

Would she want to have breakfast with him?

Last night's kiss was seared into his mind, simmering long after he'd left her house.

For a moment longer, he stood there, debating whether to walk up to her door and knock. Finally, he talked himself out of it. It was too soon after last night. After that kiss that had rocked his world. He'd see her soon enough when Monday rolled around, and he had his first day as a junior high PE teacher. By then, he'd better have his shit together and not fall all over himself when he saw her.

Valentin turned back and pushed himself harder, running faster, hoping to wear himself out and maybe free his mind of his desire to kiss Ouida Mae again. That would get him nowhere on this assignment. He needed to focus on finding the guy who'd trashed her classroom.

The sooner that happened, the sooner Bayou Mambaloa could get back to normal, and Valentin wouldn't have to herd a bunch of teenagers through PE classes.

Back at the boarding house, Valentin showered

and changed into jeans and a button-down shirt. He ran a comb through his hair and headed down to the boarding house kitchen.

Only five of the original team that had arrived in Bayou Mambaloa with Remy Montagne over a year ago remained at the boarding house. The others had found matches, gotten engaged or married, and had moved in with their partners.

Remy and Shelby were expecting a baby. Rafael and Gisele were just back from their honeymoon, and Gerard had become a farmer with his fiancée, Bernie Bellamy.

After all their years in the military, never staying in one place long enough to have lasting relationships, Valentin's buddies were settling down.

Simon Sevier was pouring a cup of coffee from the full carafe. "You were up early to run. Need a cup?"

Valentin nodded. "I do."

Simon grabbed a mug from the cabinet and poured another cup of the dark, fragrant brew. "How was your science teacher last night after her poker game?"

"She's not *my* science teacher," Valentin said as he took the mug from Simon. "She was still a little spooked by the attack. She thought she heard someone on her porch. I checked the perimeter."

"Find anything?" Simon asked over the rim of his mug.

Valentin shook his head. "No. It was dark."

"You might go back during daylight and look for footprints," Simon suggested.

That was an excellent idea and a good reason to invite himself over to Ouida Mae's that morning. "I'll do that," he said and pulled out his cell phone.

"You might wait an hour. It's still early for a Sunday morning. Most people are sleeping in or getting ready for church."

"Right." Valentin slid his cell phone back into his pocket and sipped his coffee.

"Any other thoughts on who might have trashed Miss Maudet's classroom?" Simon asked.

"No," Valentin said. It frustrated him that they didn't have any substantial clues. "All we know was that he was a male and big enough to destroy her room and sling desks around."

"And knock out Mr. Jones, a former marine." Simon's eyes narrowed. "Think it could've been a disgruntled student?"

"There aren't that many male students big enough to fit the description of the assailant."

"Not even on the football team?" Simon asked. "They grow the boys bigger these days, or so it seems."

"I could touch base with the football coach on Monday." Valentin finished his coffee, rinsed his cup and set it in the dishwasher.

"Are you ready to face a bunch of teenagers in PE class?"

Valentin shrugged. "I'd like to get my hands on Miss Sutton's lesson plans so I have half an idea of what she usually does."

"How hard could it be?" Simon waved a hand. "You can have them do some calisthenics like we did in Basic Combat Training. Pushups, sit-ups, running around the track... If you have use of the gym, have them shoot a few hoops or play volleyball.

"I thought of that."

"You do realize PE is for the students who aren't on sports teams, right?" Simon asked.

Valentin's eyebrows shot upward. "They aren't?"

"Not usually." Simon's eyes narrowed. "When I was in junior high, I played all the sports—basketball, football, baseball and soccer. PE was for the kids who weren't into sports but were required to have a physical activity on their schedule. You know, like the science nerds, computer geeks and, well, the non-athletic types."

Valentin cringed. "You're kidding, right?"

Simon shook his head. "Not the way I remember it."

"Basically, you're telling me I'll be babysitting a bunch of kids who could care less about physical training?"

Simon shrugged. "It might be different here in Bayou Mambaloa."

"But you doubt it." Valentin was beginning to dread Monday morning.

"You'll be fine," Simon assured him as he placed his cup in the dishwasher. "All you have to do is keep them moving and doing something."

Valentin was even more convinced he needed to get his hands on Miss Sutton's lesson plans. Maybe when he went to Ouida Mae's house, she could get in touch with the other teacher for him. He could arrange to meet up with her that day.

"Well, I'm headed out," Simon said. "Remy hooked me up with Mitchell Marceau down at the marina. He's taking me fishing this morning. Have a calm day before the storm." Simon waved and left the building.

Feeling a little overwhelmed, Valentin pulled out his cell phone and called Ouida Mae. "Are you up and moving?"

"I've been up for a while," she said. "Tell me something good. I could use a pick-me-up."

"Rough morning already?" he asked.

She snorted. "And I thought having my classroom trashed was bad." Her voice was low, almost a whisper.

"Could you use a little company?" he asked.

"I have some, but I'd love yours."

Valentin frowned. "You're not alone?"

"No. I have a house guest," she said.

Valentin had the feeling she wanted to say more. "Want to tell me about it?"

"Not now, but I have a pot of coffee brewing if you're interested."

"I wanted to look around your place in the daylight, and then I need your help to get ready for Monday. This PE teacher gig is all new to me."

"Come on over. I'll be here," she said.

"Is ten minutes too soon?" he asked.

"Not soon enough," she said with a sigh. "See you then."

Valentin ended the call and left the boarding house. He should have told her five minutes. With ten minutes, he'd have to drive slowly to stretch it out.

Five minutes later, he pulled into Ouida Mae's driveway. He'd sit in the truck for five more if he needed to.

He'd barely shifted into park when Ouida Mae opened the front door and came out onto the porch wearing jeans and a moss green, short sleeve pullover the same color as her eyes. She wore her auburn hair piled in a messy bun at the crown of her head. She held a cup in one hand and waved him over with the other hand, which had a white bandage wrapped around it.

He dropped down from the driver's seat, hurried up the stairs and grabbed the wrist of her bandaged hand. "What happened?"

She shrugged. "I broke a glass and cut my hand."

"Why?" He continued to hold her hand. "Did something upset you?"

She pulled her hand free and shot a glance over her shoulder. "We'll talk later," she said softly. "I have a house guest."

Valentin lowered his voice and looked over her shoulder, hoping to catch a glimpse of her guest. "When did he arrive?" His fingers curled into fists. Whoever the guest was had Ouida Mae upset.

"A few minutes after you left last night." She led the way into the house. "She's in the kitchen."

Valentin followed the science teacher down the hallway and into the kitchen, where a teenage girl stood at the stove, pushing scrambled eggs around in a skillet.

"Sophie Saulnier, this is Mr. Vachon. He's going to be the PE teacher while Miss Sutton is on a leave of absence."

Sophie turned, her forehead puckering. "Is Miss Sutton sick?"

"No," Ouida Mae said. "She's just not comfortable coming back to school until our intruder is caught."

Sophie's lips twisted, and she shook her head. "Good grief. It wasn't even her classroom—and you're going back." She lifted her chin toward Valentin. "Nice to meet you, Mr. Vachon. I'll be one of your students. I promise not to give you any trouble."

"Nice to meet you, Sophie," Valentin said. "You

were the student with Miss Maudet when her classroom was trashed, weren't you?"

She nodded. "I stayed late for help on my science homework."

"Are you doing okay?" he asked.

Sophie's gaze met Ouida Mae's. "I am."

Ouida Mae turned to Valentin with a smile. "Have you had breakfast?"

"No, ma'am, I have not," Valentin said. "I was going to ask you the same. Would you and Sophie care to join me at the local diner?"

Sophie snorted. "Hello, I'm cooking scrambled eggs. But if Miz Mo wants to eat at the diner, I'll stay here."

"I have plenty of eggs, and we cooked up enough bacon for an army if you'd like to stay and eat here," Ouida Mae said.

"As long as you let me help," Valentin said. "I know how to add a leaf to the dining table, and as long as there's only one fork, knife and spoon each, I can set a mean table."

"You're hired." Ouida Mae tipped her head toward the cabinets. "Silverware is in the top drawer to the right of the dishwasher; napkins are on the counter."

While Valentin set the table, Ouida Mae removed toast from the toaster and spread butter over the slices.

"Juice?" Valentin asked.

"In the fridge along with the milk," Ouida Mae said.

Valentin retrieved a bottle of orange juice and a carton of milk from the refrigerator and set them in the middle of the table.

Sophie scraped scrambled eggs from the skillet into a large bowl and carried it and a platter of bacon to the table.

Ouida Mae brought the stack of toast and a jar of strawberry preserves.

Valentin held out a chair for Sophie and then Ouida Mae. Once the ladies were seated, he sat next to Ouida Mae.

"Thank you for cooking, Sophie," Ouida Mae said.

"It's the least I could do since it was my fault you cut your hand." Sophie spooned eggs onto her plate and then passed the bowl to Ouida Mae.

Ouida Mae added a scoop of eggs to her plate.

"That's a story I'd like to hear," Valentin said casually.

"It's not much of one," Sophie offered. "I showed up at her back door and scared the daylights out of her." She took two slices of bacon from the platter and handed the dish to Ouida Mae.

"I wasn't expecting anyone to show up at my backdoor after midnight," Ouida Mae said. "She startled me while I was rinsing out a wine glass."

"I'll pay you for the wine glass after I sweep Mr. Parson's floors," Sophie promised.

"No need," Ouida Mae said. "It was one I picked up from a yard sale."

"Then I'll find you another," Sophie said.

"What brought you to Miss Maudet's house after midnight?" Valentin asked.

Again, Sophie's gaze met Ouida Mae's for a moment, and then she concentrated on the food on her plate. "I had an argument with my mother and needed a place to stay for the night. Miz Mo let me use her guest bedroom."

"Won't your mother be worried about you?" Valentin asked.

Sophie's fork paused halfway to her mouth. "It's complicated."

Ouida Mae laid a hand on Valentin's leg beneath the table and gave it a gentle squeeze.

He guessed it was his cue to stop asking the teen questions.

"But don't worry, I won't be here long," Sophie said. "I have to go see a friend."

"*The* friend?" Ouida Mae asked.

Sophie glanced up, nodded briefly and refocused on her food.

"I think you should wait until I get back from my morning errand," Ouida Mae said. "Just to be sure."

Sophie glanced up. Again, her gaze met Ouida Mae's as if they were sending telepathic messages or subtext Valentin was not privy to. The urge to ask what the hell was going on was overwhelming.

The hand on his leg was warm, soft and decidedly firm.

That subtext he got.

Keep your mouth shut.

He shoved another bite of eggs into his mouth rather than biting down on his tongue. As soon as he had Ouida Mae alone, he'd get his answers.

"I won't be gone long," Ouida Mae said. "Would you mind cleaning up the dishes? When I get back, we'll plan the rest of our day."

"Yes, ma'am," Sophie said, her lips tight, a crease in her brow. The girl held her fork so tightly her fingers turned white.

Ouida Mae's cell phone pinged beside her on the table. She read a text and responded, her thumbs moving briefly over the digital keyboard.

Though Valentin sat beside her, he only caught half the messages—something about a package.

Ouida Mae sent her message and turned the phone over. "That was the message I was waiting for. I need to meet a friend in ten minutes." When she started to gather her plate, Sophie held up a hand.

"Leave your dishes," the teen said. "I'll take care of them."

"I won't be gone long," Ouida Mae repeated. She turned to Valentin. "You're welcome to stay and finish your breakfast. I'll be back soon."

"I'm done," he said and pushed back from the table. "I can take you wherever you need to go."

Ouida Mae frowned. She shot a glance towards Sophie.

Sophie shrugged with more of that subtext Valentin wasn't a part of.

"I guess that will be all right," Ouida Mae said. "Are you ready?"

"Yes, ma'am." He turned to Sophie. "Are you all right here on your own?"

She nodded. "I'm used to it. Go. I'll have the dishes and the bathroom cleaned by the time you get back."

Ouida Mae gave her a reassuring smile. "Don't worry."

Sophie snorted softly. "Easy for you to say." She waved her hand. "Go."

Ouida Mae headed for the door.

Valentin hurried after her.

"Be sure to lock the door after us," Ouida Mae called out.

Sophie was right behind Valentin. "Got it."

Once Ouida Mae and Valentin were across the threshold, the door closed behind them and a clicking sound indicated the deadbolt had been engaged.

When Ouida Mae headed for her car, Valentin caught up with her. "Let me take you in my truck."

She didn't say a word but changed direction, arriving at the passenger side of his truck.

Valentin opened the door and helped her up.

Sensing her urgency, he quickly rounded the hood and slid in behind the steering wheel.

"Where to?" he asked as he backed up, turned around and drove down her driveway to the main road.

"Broussard's," she said.

He turned toward her, a frown pulling his brow downward. "Isn't the store closed on Sunday?"

She nodded, her lips tight, a frown puckering her brow. "I'm meeting Shelby Taylor in the parking lot."

Valentin drove into town to Broussard's Country Store. When he pulled into the parking lot, he drove straight up to the sheriff's deputy's vehicle. As he shifted into park, Ouida Mae shoved open the door. "I'll be right back."

He assumed she meant for him to stay in the vehicle.

Shelby eased out of her SUV with a small, brown paper bag in one hand, the other hand going to her swollen belly. She looked ready to pop. Remy was beside himself over her pregnancy and worried about her job as a deputy putting her and the baby in danger.

Valentin understood.

But Shelby was a strong, independent young woman who'd do everything in her power to protect her baby while protecting her community.

Shelby's gaze went from Ouida Mae to where Valentin sat behind the wheel.

Valentin raised a hand in greeting and lowered his window.

Shelby said something to Ouida Mae as she handed the bag over.

Ouida Mae shook her head and responded by glancing toward Valentin and saying two words in a whisper that didn't carry to his open window.

Not that he could read lips well, but it looked like she'd said *not yet.*

Valentin strained to hear what they were saying without looking too obvious. He only caught a few of Shelby's words. Something to do with *state* and *social services.* He also heard the word *mother.*

Valentin put what little he heard together and tried to make sense of the disjointed words.

If they were talking about social services, they might be discussing one of Ouida Mae's students who might need help. Since Sophie was one of Ouida Mae's students, currently staying at Ouida Mae's house, Valentin had to assume they were discussing the teenager. Maybe Shelby had tried to contact the girl's mother and social services to help place Sophie in a safer home.

All his thoughts were pure conjecture. He hoped Ouida Mae would trust him enough to bring him in on what was going on. If Sophie was in trouble, she needed protection. Since Ouida Mae had taken the teen in, that trouble might find its way to Ouida Mae as well.

If his job was to protect Ouida Mae, Valentin needed to know what was happening.

Ouida Mae nodded and said clearly, "I will." She hugged Deputy Taylor tightly, then stepped back.

The deputy waved at Valentin, climbed into her SUV and drove out of the parking lot, leaving Ouida Mae standing where they'd hugged for a moment longer.

Finally, Ouida Mae returned to Valentin's pickup and climbed in, laying the small paper bag across her lap, her bandaged hand resting over it. She stared straight ahead.

"Where to?" he asked.

She sat up straighter, squared her shoulders, and raised her chin. "Home."

He shifted into gear, turned around in the parking lot and drove to Ouida Mae's house in silence.

Valentin wanted to ask what that was all about. He wanted to ask what was wrong because, based on her body language, she was headed into dark waters or a battle that would take all of her determination.

He held his tongue. If Ouida Mae wanted him to know, she would tell him...perhaps in her own time.

At the house, he shifted into park and reached for his door handle.

Ouida Mae's hand shot out and touched his arm. "If you don't mind, give me a few minutes alone. I'll let you know when it's okay to come in—unless you have something better to do with your day."

"I don't have anything better to do. I'll wait till you're ready," he said. "Take all the time you need."

Ouida Mae gave him a weak smile and pushed open her door.

Valentin sat behind the wheel and watched as she climbed out of his truck and walked up the stairs to her house.

She stuck her key in the lock, twisted it and pushed the door open. Ouida Mae disappeared inside and closed the door behind her.

Valentin checked his watch. He sat wondering what was going on inside for a few minutes. At the five-minute mark, he remembered that he hadn't checked around her house for last night's intruder. He might as well do that now while waiting for Ouida Mae to give him the "all clear" to come into her house.

Valentin dropped down from his pickup and circled her house, looking for any signs of an intruder. He found footprints in the soft dirt behind Ouida Mae's house. Some of that dirt had been carried up the back steps in footprints. Based on the size of the footprints, they probably belonged to Sophie.

From what Ouida Mae had told him, she'd heard footsteps on the front porch the night before. Hesitant to climb the front porch steps, Valentin studied the planks on the porch for any signs of footprints there. He expanded his search, working his way outward in an ever-enlarging circle around her house.

Nothing stood out until he reached the edge of the bayou. He found a small pirogue tucked beneath a low-hanging branch and secured to a limb with a thin line. He assumed it was Sophie's.

Moving further down the edge of the bayou, he discovered a skid mark in the muddy bank where a larger skiff or boat had been pushed up onto the bank. Footprints in the mud beside the skid mark were larger than the ones he'd found on the back porch. These were man-sized footprints and had been made coming and going.

Ouida Mae had not been imagining things when she'd heard footsteps on her porch.

That worried Valentin.

Ouida Mae's home was far enough out of town to be considered isolated. It was next to another, larger home Ouida Mae had said belonged to her parents. But they were hardly over there. If she needed help, it would take time for a sheriff's vehicle to respond.

"Valentin?" Ouida Mae's voice called out.

Valentin hurried around to the front of the house to find Ouida Mae standing on the porch, a tight smile on her lips.

"Oh, there you are," she said with forced cheerfulness.

"I was just looking around the perimeter of your

yard for any indication of your other intruder last night," he said. "Everything all right?"

"Yes," she said. "Everything is going to be just fine. Isn't that right, Sophie?" She turned toward the open front door.

Sophie stood in the shadows. "Yes, ma'am," she said, her voice sounding a little choked.

Valentin nodded. Whatever was going on wasn't just fine. "It's a beautiful day; let's get out and do something."

Ouida Mae smiled. A real one this time. "That would be great. Where would you like to go?"

Since the two ladies looked a bit tense, Valentin didn't want to suggest a trip to New Orleans. Then he thought about his buddy Gerard and his fiancée, Bernadette, and a smile spread across his face. "How about I surprise you?" He held up his hands. "Don't worry; it's nothing crazy, but it will get us outdoors to enjoy the sunshine."

Ouida Mae nodded. "I could make up some sandwiches, and we could have a picnic."

"Sounds great," Valentin said. "I just need to touch base with a friend of mine. Then I'll come in and help."

"Sophie and I will get started." She went back to the house but left the front door open.

Valentin texted Gerard, asking if it would be okay for the three of them to visit for the day.

Gerard responded a moment later that it would

be fine as long as they didn't mind helping harvest vegetables Bernie needed to supply Broussard's the following morning.

Perfect. Outdoors in the sunshine, doing something productive would help anyone's spirits.

He entered the house and moved down the hallway to the kitchen, where Ouida Mae and Sophie had laid out slices of bread and were layering them with deli meat and cheese.

"Mustard or mayo?" Ouida Mae asked.

"Both," he said. "What can I help with?"

"We have the sandwiches under control," Ouida Mae responded. "You could grab a bag from the mudroom and the potato chips from the pantry, for a start."

As Valentin passed Sophie, he noted her eyes were red-rimmed, and her cheeks were tear-stained. Whatever had upset Sophie had upset Ouida Mae as well. And neither one of them wanted to talk.

Valentin would make it his challenge to bring smiles back to both of their faces. "What about drinks?" he asked.

"There's a small ice chest in the mudroom. I have a couple of sodas in the refrigerator, as well as a small bottle of apple juice. And there are some water bottles next to the ice chest in the mudroom. We can take a few of each."

Valentin filled the small ice chest with drinks and poured ice on top to keep them cool. By the time they were done, Ouida Mae and Sophie had wrapped the sandwiches and put them in the bag with the potato chips.

Valentin grabbed the small ice chest and the bag of sandwiches. "Ready?"

Ouida Mae smiled, and Sophie squared her shoulders.

"Ready," Ouida Mae said for both of them. "Where are we going?"

He grinned. "Bellamy Farms to pick vegetables."

"Sounds great," Ouida Mae said. "Right, Sophie?"

"Great," the teen agreed, with little enthusiasm. "Beats sitting around doing nothing."

Oh, good, Valentin thought. Cheering this one up would be a challenge. He looked on the bright side. He could practice his teen-handling skills on Sophie while spending more time with the pretty science teacher.

Win-Win.

CHAPTER 9

THEY RODE to Bellamy Farms in silence.

Ouida Mae went over and over in her mind the previous twenty minutes. She felt overwhelmed but knew Sophie was even more so.

Ouida Mae had to stay strong for Sophie. She wanted more than anything to confide in Valentin but didn't feel it was her right to tell Sophie's secret.

Though Ouida Mae had been fairly certain about her prognosis, she'd wanted some proof for herself and for Sophie before she looked for the right path forward.

The only person she'd confided in was Shelby Taylor. Besides being a sheriff's deputy, Shelby's connection to Broussard's country store had come in handy, considering the store was closed on Sunday. Shelby was able to get inside for the one thing they needed most to prove Ouida Mae's prediction.

Shelby had come through with an early pregnancy detection test.

Ouida Mae had helped Sophie read through the instructions before the girl had entered the bathroom, closed the door and peed on the little stick. Moments later, she'd come out, and they stood together in the hallway, watching the little stick as the results materialized.

The fifteen-year-old was pregnant.

Sophie had burst into tears.

Ouida Mae held her for a long time, telling her everything would be all right. She wasn't alone.

Though it might've been too soon for Sophie to want to leave the house, Ouida Mae knew sitting around worrying wasn't going to help. The girl needed to keep moving.

And frankly, so did Ouida Mae.

Thankfully, Valentin was willing to take them on a picnic at Bellamy Farm. At least there, they would be outdoors with a few people around them, and they'd be doing something productive.

Ouida Mae hoped it would give her time to think through the next steps they needed to take. One, Sophie needed to be under a doctor's care whether she chose to keep the baby or not; she needed somebody looking out for her own health.

Ouida Mae doubted that Sophie's mother would be of any help. The woman might be more of a hindrance than anything. She probably didn't have any health insurance since she couldn't hold down a job for any length of time. Sophie's mother needed as much help as Sophie, if not more, to get clean of drugs.

Ouida Mae wanted to ensure that Sophie didn't think this would be the end of the world for her. She had a life ahead of her and needed to stay in school. For herself and for the baby.

Ouida Mae had been to Bellamy Farms a number of times. She and Bernadette had been friends since the other woman had moved to Bayou Mambaloa after marrying her first husband, Ray Bellamy. She came to ladies' poker night when she had time. But the farm she'd inherited from her late husband took up most of her time.

Ouida Mae had gone out to help harvest vegetables when Bernie had needed help and had stayed to help can preserves and tomato sauces. She loved Bernie's old house and the smells that came from canning delicious, fresh foods. She'd expanded her business from local stores to some distributors in New Orleans.

When she and Gerard had gotten together, he'd helped on the farm when he wasn't on assignment with the Bayou Brotherhood Protectors.

Ouida Mae smiled at the memory of Gerard's first days at the Bellamy Farms. Talk about fish out of water. The man had never worked on a farm before. But he was game and had learned quickly.

Now, the two were crazy in love, when Bernie had thought she could never love another after her husband Ray had passed. It warmed Ouida Mae's heart to know her friend had been given a second chance at love. She was happy for them.

As Valentin parked in front of the farmhouse, Gerard and Bernie emerged onto the porch. Gerard had his arm around Bernie's waist. She leaned into him, her face glowing with her happiness.

Ouida Mae sighed. She'd always wanted to find someone she could love as much as her parents loved each other, and now, as much as Bernie and Gerard, Shelby and Remy, Gisele and Rafael and Lucas and Felina obviously cared about each other. It seemed all her friends were falling in love and deliriously happy.

She was happy for them and a little envious. Mostly of Shelby, who was pregnant. Soon, she'd have a baby to love.

Ouida Mae's heart pinched hard in her chest. She'd wanted someone to love and to have half a dozen babies. Growing up as an only child of loving parents, she'd dreamed of being a mother surrounded by children.

She'd been thirteen when she'd been diagnosed with endometriosis. Though she'd been treated, the doctor had told her it could impact her ability to get pregnant. She'd taken his words to heart, focused on her career and surrounded herself with children as a teacher. So far, that had been enough.

But now...

Ouida Mae sighed as she dropped down from the pickup and watched as Gerard and Bernie, so in love, greeted Valentin and Sophie. Gerard and Bernie would make great parents—and what a fabulous place to raise children. They'd have plenty of room to run and play, and they'd learn so much about nature, growing things and raising animals.

"Thank you so much for coming out to Bellamy Farms to help us with some of our harvest." Bernie hugged Ouida Mae. "It's been too long since I've had time to visit my friends."

"It has been too long," Ouida Mae said. "I should've come sooner. Though I'd like to say it was my idea to come today, it was all Valentin's doing. I can't think of a better way to spend a Sunday than in the sunshine and fresh air. We thought Sophie might enjoy coming along as well. Sophie, this is my friend Bernie Bellamy and her fiancé, Gerard Guidry."

Sophie held out her hand to Bernie. "Nice to meet you, ma'am."

Bernie smiled at Sophie and took her hand. "It's nice to meet you, too. I hope you enjoy a little hard work with your sunshine."

"A little hard work never hurt anyone," Sophie murmured.

"I like the way this young lady thinks," Gerard said.

Sophie turned to him with her hand outstretched. "Thank you. I hope I don't disappoint."

"I'm sure you won't." Gerard shook her hand with a grave expression on his face. "Nice to meet you, Sophie."

"Nice to meet you, Mr. Guidry," Sophie said.

Bernie smiled at the three of them. "Well, if you're ready, we can get started. It's best to work in the morning before it gets really hot."

"We're ready," Ouida Mae said.

The three of them followed Bernie and Gerard around the house, past the barn and into a field with row after row of different kinds of vegetables.

Bernie handed each of them a woven basket and started them down a row of zucchini and squash, showing them which ones were ripe and ready to pick, and which were overripe and should be picked and laid to the side. "I'll collect the bad ones and add them to our compost heap."

"Just this row?" Sophie asked.

Bernie chuckled. "No, there are four rows. You can each take a row of your own. When you fill the basket, bring it back to the end of the row and empty it into these cardboard boxes." She pointed to a neat stack of cardboard boxes with Bellamy acres printed on the sides.

"When we're done with the zucchini, we'll move onto the yellow squash and then the bell peppers, banana peppers and onions." Bernie raised an eyebrow in challenge. "With your help, I think we can get it done before noon. Are you up for it?"

Sophie nodded. "Yes, ma'am."

Brittany smiled at Sophie. "And you don't have to call me ma'am. My name is Bernie."

"Yes, ma'am." Sophie blushed. "I mean, Bernie."

"You can call me Gerard," Bernie's fiancé said.

Sophie frowned up at the big man. "No, thank you, sir. If you don't mind, I'll call you Mr. Guidry."

Rather than being offended, Gerard laughed. "I don't mind at all," he said with a grin. "Let's get started."

They moved slowly at first, working their way down the rows of zucchini, picking up speed as they became more confident in their abilities to choose the ripe squash. Besides picking their own rows, Bernie and Gerard answered questions, gathered the overripe and rotten squash and threw them into a wheelbarrow to be added to the compost pile at one end of the garden.

After they finished harvesting the zucchini, they moved on to the yellow squash. They stopped halfway through the morning for water and a snack of peaches straight from the tree.

Well, before noon, they finished picking the squash, peppers and onions and loaded the boxes into the back of the Bellamy Farms truck. Valentin, Ouida Mae and Sophie sat on the tailgate as Bernie drove the pickup slowly back to the house. Gerard followed on foot, pushing the wheelbarrow and stopping to dump the contents into the compost pile.

Bernie insisted on sending a box of fresh vegetables home with them. Valentin transferred the box to the back seat of the truck.

"You are staying for lunch, aren't you?" Bernie asked as they brushed the dust off their jeans.

"If you don't mind, we'd love to," Ouida Mae said. "But we brought a picnic lunch. All we need is a little shade."

"I have just the spot," Bernie said. "We have a picnic table under the old oak tree. You can set up there. I'll make some sandwiches for me and Gerard, and we'll join you. Then, when we're done, I have something I want to show you."

Ouida Mae enjoyed spending time with Gerard, Bernie, Valentin and Sophie. The guys told stories about pranks they'd played on their buddies or that had been played on them as well as describing places they'd been all over the world. Bernie talked about her plans for the farm and the products she would produce. She and Gerard were passionate about the place and its potential. Gerard and Valentin reminisced about their time in the military and the comradery they'd shared with their battle buddies.

By the time they'd finished lunch and packed away the ice chest and trash, Ouida Mae noticed that Sophie wasn't nearly as stressed or sad. Her cheeks had color, her eyes were brighter, and she'd even smiled at some of Valentin's stories.

"If you have time," Bernie said, "I promised I'd show you a surprise."

"Lead the way," Ouida Mae said.

As they followed Bernie, Valentin reached for Ouida Mae's hand. She slipped her fingers into his palm, warmth spreading across her body that had nothing to do with the air temperature. She liked holding his hand.

Ouida Mae held out her other hand to Sophie.

The teen stared down at it for a second and then gripped Ouida Mae's hand. A small smile tipped the corners of her lips. They walked this way back across the field to a pen at the far corner.

As they neared the pen, they could hear sounds of snorting.

Ouida Mae knew this to be the pig pen.

One portion of the pen was fenced off from the rest and had a low shelter at one end. Bernie opened the gate to this fenced-off area and waved a hand. "Take a look."

Sophie was first to bend and peer inside. "Oh, my goodness," she exclaimed.

Ouida Mae and Valentin bent over her shoulders to look as well.

Inside the enclosure was a huge sow lying on her side, with babies nursing on every one of her teats.

"How many are there?" Sophie asked.

Bernie grinned. "When I first counted after she had given birth, there were twelve." She pointed toward the end of the line of piglets nursing greedily. "When I came out a few hours later, there were thirteen. The little runt on the end was a surprise."

"Can I hold one?" Sophie asked.

"Sure," Bernie said. "But let me get it. I don't know how temperamental the mama will be."

Gerard caught Bernie's arm. "I'll do it," he said. "I'd rather you didn't enter the pig pen when I'm not around. And when I *am* around, I can do it for you."

"Seriously, I know what I'm doing," she protested.

"I know you do." Gerard kissed his fiancée briefly. "I'm just looking out for the both of you."

Ouida Mae shot a curious glance toward her friend. What did Gerard mean by *the both of you?*

Gerard bent his tall frame and entered the enclosure, reaching for the tiniest piglet. The baby squealed and wiggled in his hand. He backed out slowly.

The mama raised her head for a moment and laid back down, unconcerned that a human was stealing one of her babies.

Gerard straightened and handed the squirming piglet to Sophie.

The teen held the piglet in her arms, her wide eyes filling with tears. "It's so little," she said, her voice breaking. "Is it a boy or girl?" she asked as a single tear slid down her face.

Bernie leaned over and checked the piglet. "It's a girl."

More tears spilled down Sophie's cheek. "How does the mama take care of so many babies?"

Bernie chuckled. "She manages. They only nurse for around twenty-one days. Sounds a lot easier than human babies, right?" She laid a hand across her flat belly, her cheeks flushing a pretty pink.

Ouida Mae's gay met Bernie's. "Are you...?" She didn't want to say it out loud.

Bernie nodded, a smile spreading across her cheeks. "We're moving our wedding date up. What are you doing two weeks from today?"

"Going to a wedding!" Ouida Mae cried, hugged her friend and then leaned back. "How long have you known?"

"A few weeks," Bernie said as Gerard slipped an arm around her waist, grinning from ear to ear.

"When are you due?" Ouida Mae asked.

"Seven months." Bernie laughed. "Not nearly as far along as Shelby."

"You're going to have a baby," Sophie whispered.

In her happiness for her friend, Ouida Mae had forgotten how Sophie might feel about the announcement. She spun to discover the teen's face had blanched white.

Sophie shoved the piglet toward Gerard. "Take her," she said. "Please. Take her."

Gerard gathered the squealing piglet, his brow denting in concern. "What's wrong?"

Bernie reached for Sophie. "Did it hurt you?"

"No. I just—" The girl brushed past Bernie, dodged Ouida Mae and ran all the way back to the house.

Ouida Mae touched Bernie's arm. "I'm sorry, but we need to go." She smiled tightly at Bernie and Gerard. "I'm so happy for you both. Thank you for letting us spend the day with you."

When Ouida Mae started for the house, Bernie called after her. "Let me pay you for your time and effort."

Ouida Mae looked back over her shoulder. "That's not necessary. I loved helping."

Bernie hurried over to hand her a few twenties. "I figured you would say that but at least give this to Sophie and tell her thank you. I'm sorry if I said or did anything to upset her."

Ouida Mae hugged her friend again. "You didn't. She's going through a hard time right now."

"She's a sweet girl," Bernie said. "I hope everything works out for her."

"If you or she need help, call us," Gerard said, coming to stand beside Bernie.

"Day or night," Bernie added.

Tears welled in Ouida Mae's eyes. "Thank you."

Valentin shook Gerard's hand and hugged Bernie.

"Congratulations." He reached for Ouida Mae's hand and ran across the field with her.

"What's wrong with Sophie?" he asked.

"It's not my story to tell," Ouida Mae said, breathing hard as she ate the distance in her short strides.

"She's pregnant, isn't she?" he said.

Ouida Mae stumbled.

Valentin let go of her hand and gripped her arm, steadying her.

"She didn't want anyone to know." Ouida Mae stared up into Valentin's face. "I promised not to tell."

"I won't let her know that I know," he assured her, moving again beside her at a slower pace. "Besides, you didn't tell me. I figured it out on my own." He winked at Ouida Mae. "She's a good kid. We'll help her figure this out."

Ouida Mae's heart warmed at his words, including himself in finding a solution. But first, they had to catch up to the teen.

"I hope she didn't run away," Ouida Mae said.

"If she did," Valentin said, "we'll find her."

Ouida Mae heaved a winded sigh when they found Sophie in the back seat of the truck, her face buried in her hands.

Ouida Mae slid into the back seat with the traumatized girl and wrapped an arm around her shoulders. "Honey, you're going to be all right."

Sophie buried her face in Ouida Mae's neck. "How can I be? I've messed up everything."

"No, you haven't, sweetie. I'll help you." Ouida Mae hugged her tighter.

"We'll both help you with whatever you need," Valentin promised as he closed the door behind them. He climbed into the driver's seat and headed back to Ouida Mae's house.

They were driving through town when Ouida Mae's cell phone pinged with an incoming text. She couldn't reach it where she'd left it in the front console and didn't care. Sophie needed her comfort more than Ouida Mae needed to respond to a text.

At the same time, Valentin's phone chirped. He pulled to the side of the road and read the message, cursing quietly beneath his breath.

"What?" Ouida Mae asked, dread building in her gut.

"It's from Principal Ashcraft. The school board has called an emergency meeting. It's taking place now at the school. She wants both of us there ASAP."

Ouida Mae's arms tightened around the pregnant teen. "They can wait until we get Sophie back to the house."

Sophie leaned back and scrubbed her hands over her face. "No, Miz Mo. You have to be there. I heard about what the protestors did while you were trying to fix up your classroom. You need to be there to defend yourself. Don't let them push you around."

Ouida Mae grinned at Sophie. "Listen to you being all protective. That's the independent young woman in you. But I'd feel better if I got you safely to my house first."

"But they might make decisions without your input," Sophie took her hand. "I couldn't live with myself if you weren't there, and they did anything to hurt you or your job as a teacher. You're the best teacher in that school."

Valentin slowed at the turn that would take them straight to the school. "What's it to be, Miz Mo?"

Sophie answered for her. "The school." She met and held Ouida Mae's gaze.

Still, Valentin didn't make that turn yet.

Ouida Mae drew in a deep breath. "What Sophie said."

Valentin made the turn, sending his truck toward the junior high.

The parking lot was filling quickly as teachers, parents, and even students, streamed into the gymnasium.

Valentin parked his truck in the grass and hurried around to open the door for Ouida Mae.

As she got out of the truck, Sophie did, too.

Ouida Mae shook her head. "You might want to stay in the truck."

"I'm going with you," Sophie said. "It's not just parents and teachers. Half the students are here as well. I want to be here. This is my school.

Ouida Mae nodded. "You have a right to be here. But if this is an attack on me, you might not want to stand too close." She gave her a crooked smile.

"Miz Mo, you were here for me. I'm here for you." The girl hooked her arm through Ouida Mae's and marched toward the school, her face set in determined lines.

Sophie might be a teenager and pregnant, but she was one tough cookie. Ouida Mae's heart swelled with pride for the girl. If she ever had children, she'd want them to be like Sophie.

With Valentin on one side and Sophie on the other, they entered the gymnasium and stood for a moment to get their bearings.

Deputy Shelby Taylor stood near the entrance.

Ouida Mae met her gaze. "Any idea what this is about?"

Her friend shrugged. "I just got here, too. The sheriff and Remy are on their way in case we need backup."

"Good grief," Ouida Mae said. "I certainly hope we don't need it."

Shelby tilted her head toward the full bleachers. "You never know what will happen."

Principal Ashcraft hurried over.

Sophie disengaged her arm from Ouida Mae's and took a small step back. "I've got your back," she whispered.

"Oh, good, you're here," Principal Ashcraft said.

"The parent-teacher association went behind my back and called the school board for an emergency meeting. Apparently, word spread like wildfire, and all the parents decided to show up. When the kids heard about it, they started texting each other and decided to show up as well. There are no rules saying that the children cannot be present at a school board meeting." The principal waved a hand at the quickly filling bleachers in the gymnasium. "We don't even fill the bleachers for a basketball game." She faced Ouida Mae. "And yes, I suspect it has to do with you, Miss Maudet."

Ouida Mae lifted her chin. "What do they want?"

"We're about to find out," Principal Ashcraft said. "We set up chairs and tables for the school board and reserved seating in the bleachers across from them for the teachers and admin staff. You and Mr. Vachon should come sit with us."

Ouida Mae hesitated.

Sophie leaned toward her and whispered in her ear, "Go. I'll be nearby."

Ouida Mae didn't like leaving the teenager like she was the one on trial with the school board in this situation. She went with Principal Ashcraft and Valentin and settled on the bottom row of the bleachers, facing the panel of board members.

CHAPTER 10

VALENTIN SAT on one side of Ouida Mae; Principal Ashcraft sat on the other.

The president of the school board tapped a small wooden gavel on the table in front of him. "Quiet, please," he said. In a more commanding voice, he repeated, "Quiet!"

People in the bleachers settled and stopped talking. Valentin glanced around the gymnasium, amazed at the people who'd gathered. The rows of bleachers that had been reserved for the teachers were filled. Parents had filled in behind them. Students flanked either side of the parents.

Several parents stood near the tables where the school board had taken up residence. One of those parents was Katherine Edouard. She wore a dress and conservative heels, her face expertly made up, not too much, but enough to enhance her features.

She'd pulled her hair up in a loose bun, and her lips were pressed into a thin, disapproving line as she stared at Ouida Mae, who'd arrived in what she'd worn to pick vegetables all morning in a garden.

Ouida Mae's jeans and shirt were dusty, and she had streaks of dirt on her otherwise makeup-free face and beneath her fingernails. She'd secured her pretty auburn hair in a girlish ponytail and looked adorable to Valentin, but the school board might not see her as adorable as he did.

"Wish I'd had time for a shower," Ouida Mae whispered, rubbing her hands against her jeans.

"Don't worry," Valentin said. "A little dirt on your cheeks makes you look badass."

She raised her hand quickly to her cheek. "I have dirt on my face?"

The president of the school board smacked his gavel on the table once more. "Let's bring this emergency meeting of the Bayou Mambaloa School Board to order. We were notified this morning that an emergency meeting needed to be conducted and that it was a matter of life and death. This better be good. I'm missing my football game for this. Mrs. Katherine Edouard, since you initiated this meeting, you have the floor."

Katherine Edouard stepped forward. "President Ford, as you are well aware, our school was attacked on Friday afternoon—specifically, Miss Maudet's room."

She laid eight by ten photographs in front of the school board, spreading them across the tables so that all members of the board could see them. "As you can see from the pictures I took shortly after the attack, it is plain to even the least intelligent observer that the attack was in protest against the science teacher's proposed curriculum."

"We've seen these photographs," President Ford acknowledged. "What is your point?"

She laid another photograph in front of the school board president. "This is a picture of poor Mr. Jones, who was brutally attacked in that classroom. He could've been killed and sadly remains in a coma," she stated.

"Again, Ms. Edouard, the school board is aware of the situation," the school board president said. "Could you please get to the point?"

Ms. Edouard's eyes narrowed. "None of this would've happened if Miss Maudet hadn't insisted on filling our impressionable young students' minds with things that should not be taught in school. Some things are better taught at home. Teaching young people about S.E.X. is criminal. It will plant ideas in their minds that they are not ready to understand."

A voice from the student section of the bleachers half-coughed, half-shouted, "Bullshit!" Laughter erupted from the students and some of the parents.

Ms. Edouard glared up at the students. "You might laugh and think that's funny, but because Miss

Maudet's proposed curriculum and the mention of sex education, it planted seeds in their young minds."

Principal Ashcraft stood. "It takes more than planting seeds in a student's mind for one to get pregnant."

"I have the floor." Katherine Edouard stared down her nose at the principal. "You'll have to wait your turn."

"Ms. Edouard," the school board president said, "people don't get pregnant from planting seeds in minds. What is the life-or-death reason for which you've called us here today?"

"I'd gladly tell you if I could continue uninterrupted," Katherine said. She waited for the gymnasium to quieten down. "My point is this school is not safe for our students as long as Miss Maudet is a part of the teaching staff. She should not be allowed back in the school with her progressive curriculum that is poisoning the minds of our children."

The gymnasium erupted in a rush of murmured protests and several parents shouting above them, "Hear! Hear!"

The school board president banged his gavel on the table. "Quiet, please!" Once the audience was sufficiently silent, President Ford said, "It is my understanding that the sex education portion of Miss Maudet's curriculum was only to be presented to students whose parents had not opted out of having their student receive this information. The school board also reviewed what Miss Maudet had planned to teach in her sex education course. We all agreed it was valuable information for young people to receive, as long as their parents did not object."

Katherine lifted her chin higher. "Am I to understand that the school board reviewed and approved this curriculum without consulting parents first?"

"No, we did not review and approve this curriculum without consulting parents first," one of the other school board members spoke up. "We had a focus group review it with us. We were in one-hundred percent agreement that this information be presented."

Katherine planted a fist on one of her hips. "And why was I, the president of the parent-teacher association, not included in this focus group?"

"We used a random selection of parents," the school board member replied.

"Ms. Edouard," the school board president said, "if your primary purpose for calling this meeting was to fire Miss Maudet, that is not going to happen. It's hard enough to find qualified teachers willing to work in small towns like Bayou Mambaloa. Miss Maudet is an exemplary teacher who cares about her students enough to provide a curriculum that will help them make better choices. However, because of the recent incident, Principal Ashcraft has placed a moratorium on the sex education curriculum. We will revisit that curriculum later in the semester.

Now, if that is all you have to say, does anyone else have a life-or-death reason for this meeting to continue?"

Katherine Edouard's cheeks turned a ruddy red beneath her perfectly applied makeup. "I'm not finished. Whoever attacked her classroom may return as long as she still works at this school. That places our students in danger. Not only that, but the suggestion of her sex education curriculum has also already had a negative impact on one of our students. Because of Miss Maudet's blatant disregard for the easily impressed minds of our students, one of our own is now pregnant."

Ouida Mae tensed beside Valentin.

Valentin's gut clenched as Katherine Edouard spun and pointed her finger at Sophie.

"Oh no." Ouida Mae was halfway out of her seat when Katherine spun and pointed at Sophie.

There was no stopping Katherine's tirade. "Sophie Saulnier, one of our poor girls, is pregnant at the tender age of fourteen."

Everyone in the gymnasium seemed to gasp as one. All eyes shifted to Sophie.

Ouida Mae and Valentin rushed toward her.

Behind them, Katherine continued spewing words. "This would not have happened if Miss Maudet hadn't insisted on teaching sex education in the classroom. I demand she be fired today."

Before Valentin and Ouida Mae could reach Sophie, the girl darted for the door.

Thankfully, Shelby was there. She wrapped her arm around the girl and escorted her out of the gymnasium.

Shouts erupted throughout the audience. The school board president banged his gavel continuously, shouting for quiet.

Valentin and Ouida Mae left the chaos behind and hurried out to find Sophie in Shelby's arms, standing at the far end of the parking lot beside Valentin's truck. The teenager's body shook with heart-wrenching sobs.

"Oh, Sophie." Ouida Mae held her arms open. "I'm so sorry. I didn't tell her. None of the people who knew would have shared that information."

"It's all my fault," Sophie turned and fell into Ouida Mae's arms. "I never should've trusted him."

"Trusted who?"

"My boyfriend," she sobbed.

"Who is your boyfriend?"

"Sophie," a voice called out behind Valentin. "I'm sorry. Oh, baby, I'm so sorry."

Everyone spun toward the voice.

A young man stood with his arms at his sides, his forehead dented in a tortured crease. "She was going after Miz Mo. I told her the kids at our school needed Miz Mo's class to understand what happens when they do it without protection—that things can happen to anyone. That it had happened already. That someone in our class was pregnant and might not have been had she had Miz Mo's class."

Sophie flung herself at the boy, pounding her fists against his chest. "You told her? How could you! I hate you! I hate you!"

He wrapped his arms around her, trapping her hands between them. "I didn't say who was pregnant," he said. "She guessed."

"Does she know it was you?" Sophie demanded.

Chase didn't respond.

"Does she know it was you?" Sophie leaned back and stared up into his face. "She doesn't."

His arms fell to his sides. "She thinks we broke up three months ago. I got tired of hearing her say you were a blemish on my father's reelection campaign."

Sophie backed away from him. "In other words, I'm an embarrassment to you and your family." She lifted her chin. "I never want to see you again."

Chase stepped forward. "But Sophie, I love you."

With the amount of pain in Chase's voice, Valentin could tell the boy believed what he said. On the other hand, he'd thrown Sophie under the bus when he'd told his mother.

Valentin faced Sophie. "Are you ready to leave?"

She turned her back on Chase. "I am."

He helped her up into the truck. When he tried to close the door, Chase's hand reached out and stopped him.

"Sophie, I'm sorry for everything. I want to do right by you and the baby. Marry me, Sophie. I'll figure out how to take care of you and the baby. I swear on my life, I love you."

Sophie reached out and pulled the door closed between them, refusing to look in his direction.

"Sophie!" Chase laid his hand on the window. "I never meant to hurt you."

Valentin stepped between Chase and his truck. "You need to leave."

"But—"

Valentin shook his head. "Now."

Ouida Mae touched the boy's arm. "You've done enough. Let her go," she said softly.

Chase stepped back. "Can't you see?" Tears welled in his eyes. "I love her."

"Then give her the space she needs," Ouida Mae said.

He met Ouida Mae's gaze and finally nodded. "I will. For now. But I'm not giving up on her."

He focused on Sophie. "Your mother might have given up on you, but I'm not, Sophie."

The young man spun on his heels. Instead of returning to the gym, he walked away from the school.

Ouida Mae turned to Shelby. "I'm worried about him."

Shelby nodded. "I'll follow him to make sure he gets home safely."

"Thank you, Shelby," Ouida Mae said.

Valentin opened the back door for Ouida Mae to climb in with Sophie.

The teen didn't scoot over to make room. "You don't need to sit with me," she said. "I'm all right."

Ouida Mae stared up at her. "Are you sure?"

Sophie snorted softly. "I can take care of myself. I've been doing it for years."

"Sophie, you're not alone anymore," Ouida Mae said. "I'll help you in any way I can."

"I appreciate everything you've done for me, Miz Mo." She gave Ouida Mae a weak smile. "But I know the only person who can truly help me is me. Can we leave now? I'm really tired."

"Sophie, I'm not giving up on you or letting you do this all on your own."

"Please," the girl said, "I'd like to leave before everyone comes out of the gym."

Ouida Mae nodded. "Okay. Let's go home."

Valentin held Ouida Mae's door open for her and helped her up into the passenger seat. Thankfully, no one emerged from the gym as they pulled out of the parking lot. The drive back to Ouida Mae's was made in complete silence.

Ouida Mae stared out the window without blinking, worry knitting her brow.

Sophie's reflection in the rearview mirror was stoney as she faced the side window.

When they arrived back at Ouida Mae's house,

Sophie pushed open her door before Valentin could shift into Park. She dropped to the ground and ran toward the bayou.

Ouida Mae shoved her door open immediately and went after the girl. "Sophie! Wait!"

Valentin shifted into park, shut off the engine and went after the two women.

Sophie was headed for her pirogue. If she reached it before they caught up with her, she would disappear into the bayou. By the time they found a boat to go after her, she could be anywhere.

Valentin raced past Ouida Mae and caught up with Sophie as she struggled to untie the line holding her pirogue to the tree limb. He wrapped his arms around her from behind.

"Let go of me," Sophie cried.

"I can't," Valentin said. "You can't run away from your problems. They follow you and force you to deal with them. If I let you go, you'll only be running away. I think you're a great kid, and I don't want you to get hurt."

Her body sagged against his and shook with silent sobs. "T-they know. Everyone knows."

Ouida Mae caught up, breathing hard. "So what?" she said and bent over, placing her hands on her knees. "It was only going to be a matter of time. A pregnancy is hard to hide." When she had her breathing under control, she straightened. "I know you feel like your whole world is falling apart. But trust me, it won't if you don't let it. You've been taking care of yourself for so long that you can handle this."

Valentin loosened his hold on Sophie and let his hands drop to his sides. "Miz Mo's right. Besides, what would you have accomplished by taking off into the bayou?"

"I could disappear," she whispered. "No one would miss me."

"You're wrong," Ouida Mae said, drawing the girl into her arms. "I've always admired you as a student. The more I get to know you, the more I love who you are."

Sophie looked up into Ouida Mae's eyes. "Why? I'm not pretty. I'm only an average student. I freaked out holding a piglet. What does that say about me?"

Ouida Mae smiled and brushed the strand of hair out of Sophie's face. "You're scared. You've been living in a shack without running water or electricity, and you haven't had anybody tell you how beautiful and important you are for too long."

Sophie's brimmed with tears. "He brought me food and blankets and helped me clean up the shack. He said he loved me and told me I was beautiful." Tears slipped down her cheeks. "The one person I trusted most, and he lied."

Ouida Mae gathered Sophie in her arms. "You're a strong young woman. You'll make it through all this."

"Why should I even try? Everything I do ends in failure. I just want to die."

Valentin's chest tightened at the anguish in Sophie's voice.

"No, sweetie, you can't think that way. You have your whole life ahead of you. Your baby needs you to survive so she can live."

"But if I die, she won't have to live knowing her mother was a loser like her mother before her."

"You aren't a loser. You don't take drugs. I've never seen you hurt another person. You work hard in school to make a better life for yourself."

"If I have this baby, I can't finish school or go to college. I can't bring a baby to the shack. I can't even get a job until I'm sixteen, and I won't have a place for us to stay."

"You've only just learned you're pregnant," Ouida Mae said. "We need to get you to a doctor and a counselor to discuss your options. You don't have to keep the baby."

Sophie pressed a hand to her belly. "I won't go for an abortion. I can barely squash a spider. I couldn't kill a baby."

"I didn't necessarily mean abortion," Ouida Mae said softly. "There are plenty of people who can't have babies who would give anything to raise yours. Women like me, who have reproductive issues that could keep them from getting pregnant." She smiled. "Your baby could find a home with parents who could give her a beautiful, happy life." She cupped Sophie's face in her palm. "And you could finish school, go to college and have a family when you're ready."

Ouida Mae wrapped her arm around Sophie's shoulders and steered her toward the house. "Let's make dinner. We all make better decisions on a full stomach."

Valentin fell in step behind them.

"You don't have to do this," Sophie said.

"Do what?" Ouida Mae asked. "Make dinner? Yes, I do. I'm hungry, and I'll bet you and Mr. Vachon are, too." She shot a smile over her shoulder at Valentin. "Am I right?"

"Absolutely," he said with a grin.

"Not dinner," Sophie said. "Everything. Giving me a place to stay, feeding me, taking me to Bellamy Farms... Why are you doing this?"

"Because I love you, Sophie. You're a kind and beautiful person."

"I'm not pretty," she argued.

"You are beautiful—inside where it counts and outside as well."

Sophie stopped as they reached the porch steps. "I can't go back to school. They'll stare at me, call me a slut and make fun of the girl who was stupid enough to get pregnant."

"You're a strong and independent young woman," Ouida Mae said.

"Sophie, everyone makes mistakes," Valentin said. "It takes courage to keep going despite them. You've been living alone in the bayou. That takes an incredible amount of courage."

Sophie frowned. "Yeah, but there wasn't anyone out there to call me names or judge me."

"They're playing the short game," Valentin said. "You have to focus on the long game. Junior high and high school don't last forever. Look to your future beyond high school and remember that the best revenge is your own success."

"That's right," Ouida Mae said. "Stay in school, go to college and become your most successful self. You won't even remember the kids poking fun at you today."

"Now, about dinner…" Valentin tipped his head toward his truck. "We have fresh vegetables we can cut up to stir fry."

"I have some chicken we can throw on the grill," Ouida Mae said.

"Perfect," Valentin said. "I'm a master grillsman."

Ouida Mae laughed. "Is that a real thing?"

"I'll be teaching PE, not English," Valentin winked. "Just go with it, and I'll take care of the chicken."

Ouida Mae grinned. "Grillsman it is." She hooked her arm through Sophie's elbow and marched her inside.

Tomorrow might be a difficult day for Sophie, but

Ouida Mae was determined to make the rest of the day happy for the girl.

Valentin followed. He was beginning to understand what made Ouida Mae a great teacher. She had a big heart, compassion and empathy for others. Her students loved her because she loved them.

Damned if he wasn't falling in love with her as well.

CHAPTER 11

Ouida Mae helped Sophie get ready for school the next morning, making sure the girl looked her best and hoping it would give her some of the confidence she'd need to get through the day.

"Keep your chin up. You haven't done anything they haven't done or thought about doing. You just didn't know to prepare properly." Ouida Mae winked at Sophie. "If you get overwhelmed, go to the nurse's office and lie down. I'll let her know I told you that you could." She smiled and turned Sophie toward the mirror. "Whoever made you believe you weren't pretty was dead wrong. Look at yourself. You're a beautiful young woman."

Sophie raised a hand to the shiny brown curls framing her face. "How did you make my hair do that?"

"I've had years of practice taming my red waves. They're not nearly as lovely as your rich brown curls. Sometimes, you have to scrunch them just to get them to be their best."

Sophie smoothed her hands over the pale pink ribbed knit shirt Ouida Mae had given her to wear with a pair of stone-washed jeans and white canvas sneakers. "Thank you for the loan of your clothes and shoes."

"They aren't a loan," Ouida Mae insisted. "If you like them enough, they're yours to keep. Are you going to be all right in those shoes? They looked a little tight."

"They aren't too tight."

"Good." Ouida Mae smiled. "I was going to donate them because they were too big for me."

"I like them," Sophie said. "And the shirt and jeans. Thank you." She stared at herself in the mirror, her brow wrinkling. "I don't know if I can do this."

Ouida Mae wrapped an arm around her waist and met her gaze in the mirror. "Take it one day at a time. I'm there all day if you need me—and so is Mr. Vachon."

She gave a brief smile. "I have both of you for at least one hour each."

"That's right. That leaves only six hours in other classes and lunch." Ouida Mae hugged her tighter. "You can do this."

Sophie gave herself a battle-ready nod and lifted her chin. "I can do this."

As she climbed into the passenger seat of Ouida Mae's car, her chin dipped, and a worried frown creased her forehead.

Ouida Mae drove to the school and into the parking lot, unsure of how things had gone with the school board the day before. She'd received two texts after the board meeting concluded. One from Principal Ashcraft, saying *We'll see you at school on Monday.* The second text had been from Shelby saying, *Congratulations, you are loved. Principal Ashcraft will fill you in on Monday.*

After listening to Katherine Edouard's rant about how sex education was poisoning students' minds, Ouida Mae was glad she'd left when she had.

She walked in through the front entrance with Sophie at her side. "You're going to be okay," she said as she turned toward her classroom, and Sophie turned toward her first-hour class.

The girl walked with her chin up and her back stiff. As she had predicted, some of the other students pointed and whispered to each other.

Ouida Mae wished she could shield Sophie from their comments and ridicule, but the sooner Sophie learned to deal with her situation, the better.

Principal Ashcraft came out of her office with a smug smile. "The good news is you still have a job."

Her lips twisted. "The bad news is you still have a job." She winked. "Do you know how hard it is to find a good science teacher?"

Ouida Mae shook her head.

"I do," Principal Ashcraft said. "And when you find a good one, you hold on tight." She hugged Ouida Mae. "Now, get to work."

Ouida Mae ducked into the nurse's office to let her know about Sophie and then hurried toward her freshly painted classroom. The attack on her room seemed to have occurred weeks rather than days earlier. Sophie's problems had taken all of Ouida Mae's focus.

As she passed other teachers in the hallway, Ouida Mae was surprised at the smiles and comments.

"Wow, Miz Mo, you missed a good meeting," the math teacher said.

"You should be proud of your students," the art teacher said. "They love you."

When she arrived at Ms. Durrand's door, her friend wrapped her arms around her and hugged her tightly. "You left too early. Every student in the gymnasium went to bat for you, along with three-quarters of the parents and every teacher. The only ones with a gripe against you were Katherine Edouard and her group of mean-girl mamas." Ms. Durrand grinned. "Not only did the school board nix the idea of firing you, but they also asked that your

sex education course be put back on the schedule—
the sooner, the better."

"That's wonderful," Ouida Mae said, glad things
had worked out for her but still worried about
Sophie.

Ms. Durrand frowned. "I would think you'd be a
little happier your school stuck up for you."

"I am," Ouida Mae said. "I just wish the students
could all be empathetic to Sophie. It's hard enough
being a pregnant teen. She doesn't need to be bullied
and ostracized by her classmates."

Ms. Durrand nodded. "I'll keep an eye out for her.
It's really great of you to take her in. I understand her
mother is of no help."

"She's better off with me, at least for now. I'm not
sure what will happen when Child Protective
Services gets their hands on her. She doesn't want to
go into foster care."

"I can't blame her. She could end up anywhere
else in Louisiana. This is her hometown and her
school."

Ouida Mae nodded. "She needs a stable environ-
ment, now more than ever."

"Have you thought of being her foster parent?"

"I understand it takes a lot of paperwork and time
to be accepted into the program." Ouida Mae glanced
down the hallway where the pregnant teen had
disappeared into a classroom. "While I weed through

bureaucratic red tape, what will happen to Sophie in the meantime?"

"You need somebody to champion your cause and push the red tape through quickly," Ms. Durrand said.

Ouida Mae gave her a crooked smile. "Do you know anybody who can do that?"

Ms. Durrand sighed. "I wish I did." She glanced down the hallway, and her eyes widened. "Wow, the scenery is going to be a lot better around here." She tipped her head toward the office.

Valentin stood with Principal Ashcraft, dressed in dark, tailored slacks and a short-sleeved, white button-down shirt, with his dark hair slicked back and his beard neatly trimmed. The man made Ouida Mae's heart flutter and her knees go weak. Yes, indeed, the scenery had improved significantly.

He faced her direction and gave her a brief nod and a smile.

Ouida Mae couldn't hold back her own smile. During dinner the night before, she'd gone over what little she knew about the PE program, ending with the advice to just keep them moving. Busy teenagers were less likely to get into trouble.

The first bell rang.

Ouida Mae dragged her gaze away from Valentin and hurried into her classroom, wondering if the PE teacher would swing by her place later that evening. She had been sure to mention they had enough leftovers for another full meal if he cared to join them the next night.

He hadn't actually committed to dinner with them, but he also hadn't declined.

Ouida Mae might be foolish to hold out hope that he would join them again, but she couldn't help it. She liked his company, and so did Sophie.

Throughout the day, she wondered how Valentin was handling the teenagers in his PE and Gifted and Talented classes. If he came to dinner, she'd find out.

VALENTIN HURRIED to the gymnasium to change into clothing more suitable for working out. Principal Ashcraft had kept him longer than he had anticipated. He'd wanted to make a good impression on the first day by wearing nice clothes. In the future, he'd come to work dressed ready to go to work in a tracksuit and tennis shoes.

He arrived in the male locker room in time to find two bigger boys pushing around a skinny kid wearing glasses. The little guy had been changing into his PE uniform shorts and a T-shirt. The bigger guys shoved him against a locker.

Apparently, they hadn't seen the PE teacher enter the locker room.

Valentin cleared his throat, capturing their attention.

Immediately, the big guy released the skinny one's shirt and stepped back.

"Anyone want to tell me what's going on?"

The big guy crossed his arms over his chest and shook his head.

The skinny kid straightened the hem of his shirt and opened his mouth.

One harsh look from the big guy, and the skinny kid shut his mouth.

"Are all of you in the PE class this morning?" Valentin asked.

The big guy shook his head. "Nope. We were just leaving." As he passed the little guy, he bumped his shoulder into him, knocking him backward into the metal lockers.

Valentin didn't have to be a rocket scientist to recognize when a kid was being bullied. However, he also knew having a teacher demand an apology from the bully wouldn't solve the problem. The skinny guy needed some lessons on how to defend himself against bullies.

Once the bullies left the locker room, Valentin met the skinny guy's four-eyed gaze. "Are you all right?"

The skinny guy shrugged and rubbed his shoulder.

"Does that guy do that often?" Valentin asked.

"Every day, sometimes twice a day," the boy muttered.

Valentin held out his hand. "I'm the new PE teacher, Mr. Vachon, and you are?"

The kid laid his limp hand in Valentin's grip. "Nigel Owens."

Valentin gripped the kid's hand. "Lesson one in dealing with a bully is to give a firm handshake."

"How will that help?"

"Shows you have confidence." He nodded toward their joined hands. "Show me what you've got."

The teen squeezed, but not enough to squish a fly.

"Squeeze like you do when you open a jar for the first time," Valentin said.

The boy's grip tightened.

"Better," Valentin said, even though the amount of force the kid put into it wouldn't open any jar he'd ever worked with. "We'll work on that with some strength training."

Nigel blinked up at him through his glasses. "Huh?"

If Nigel was a prime example of the rest of the kids in PE class, Simon had been spot-on with his description. What did Valentin know about motivating teens who could care less about getting physical?

"Look, I need to change. Go out there and let the others know I'll only be a couple of minutes."

"Uh, yeah. Okay."

"The correct response is 'yes, sir,'" Valentin said.

"Uh, yes, sir?"

"Say it like you mean it."

"Yes, sir," the boy said with even less enthusiasm.

"Now, go."

The kid hurried out of the locker room.

As he flung off his first-impression clothes, Valentin muttered, "And I left the Navy so I wouldn't have to train recruits who were wet behind their ears."

In less than two minutes, he entered the gym dressed in the only tracksuit he'd ever owned, the one he'd been issued as a new Navy recruit a million years ago. It had been in the storage unit he'd rented for years and finally cleared out before he'd made the move to Louisiana. Navy blue with NAVY written across the left breast in bright yellow, it was tight across the shoulders and a bit faded from age, not use. He preferred to wear shorts and a T-shirt when he worked out.

A rag-tag group of students sat on the bottom row of the bleachers, looking as enthusiastic as a yard dog on a hot day.

Valentin had his work cut out for him. He channeled his favorite drill instructor from basic Navy training and stood tall. "Good morning, ladies and gentlemen. I'm your new PE teacher, Mr. Vachon. You can call me Mr. Vachon or Sir."

"Are you kidding?" A tubby kid with his lip curled up on one side lounged on the bench, his shirt hanging out and his socks sagging around his ankles.

"I assure you I am not," Valentin said. "Sit up straight and tuck your T-shirt into your shorts."

The boy slowly sat up. "Where's Ms. Sutton?"

"Not here. I'm your new PE teacher. We'll do physical training my way. We will work and train as a team. If one member of the team slacks off or causes problems, the entire team does pushups. If you can't complete all of your pushups during class, you will report to the gym after school to finish. *As. A. Team.*"

The group of students groaned.

"This isn't the Navy," the big kid said.

"Obviously," Valentin said. "But with determination and teamwork, any one of you could join the Navy and serve your country."

"What if we don't want to join the Navy?" Big kid asked.

"You don't have to, but you will have the confidence and physical ability to make that choice instead of having the choice made for you, barring you from service."

Seeing that he wasn't getting through to them, he changed tactics. "How many of you are tired of bullies picking on you and your friends?"

More than half of the students raised a hand. The others sat quietly, looking afraid of their own shadows.

"Quite a few," Valentin said with a nod. "If you work hard and respect your teammates, I'll show you some self-defense techniques you can use the next time a bully tries to push you around."

"What if the bully is twice your size," Nigel asked.

Valentin met the skinny kid's gaze. "The techniques work no matter the size of the aggressor." He looked around at the boys and girls.

"It'll never work," Big Guy said.

"You'll never know if you don't try." The lack of enthusiasm was killing him. "Give yourself a week doing things my way. If you don't see improvement, I'll come to school dressed as your choice of a cosplay character."

"Make it Harley Quinn, and you got a deal," Big Guy said.

The group of teens laughed. Some nodded.

"Yeah, make it Harley," a tall, painfully thin boy called out.

Valentin arched an eyebrow. "On the flip side of that promise, you all have to have skin in the game."

When they all looked at him as if they didn't understand, he clarified. "You have to give it your best effort as a team. If any *one* of you doesn't, *all* of you have to come to school dressed as Harley Quinn. Is it a deal?"

"Deal," Nigel was first to say. "I want to know how to deal with the bullies. I'm sick and tired of being shoved into lockers or tossed into the trash bin out back."

Several others murmured agreement.

"As a team, do I hear you're in?"

Some kids nodded.

Others murmured, "Sure."

A couple said, "Yeah."

He stood at attention and projected his voice like a drill instructor. "That's *yes, sir!*"

"Yes, sir," the group of kids said.

"I can't hear you," he called out.

"Yes, sir," they said a little louder.

"Principal Ashcraft can't hear you," he said.

By now, the teens were on their feet. As one, they shouted, "Yes, sir!"

"Go, team!" Valentin shouted.

Over the remainder of the hour, he showed the students how to line up in formation, stand at attention or parade rest and how to perform basic marching movements. He assigned four squad leaders. A short girl named Abby, Nigel, a tall, heavyset girl named Stella and the big guy, Herschel.

By the end of the hour, they looked pretty good for new recruits. The quiet group of students left the gymnasium, all talking at once.

Valentin drew a deep breath and let it out slowly. One PE class down, four to go and one Gifted and Talented class he had no clue how to handle. He made the same agreement for the next two PE classes, getting buy-in from the students. By the end of each class, they knew how to fall into formation, stand at attention, forward march, halt and perform an about-face. For homework, they were to practice what they'd learned and come back the next day even better.

He was glad to take a break at lunch and join the other teachers in the teacher's lounge. As soon as he entered the room, he scanned the faces until he found Ouida Mae. She smiled when his gaze met hers. She nodded toward the empty chair beside hers.

He waded through the room and was stopped several times by teachers eager to meet him. When he finally reached Ouida Mae's table, he sank into his seat. "Hey," he said. "How's your day going? Principal Ashcraft told me the school board backed you one hundred percent, to include reinstating your sex education class." He grinned. "That's great, right?"

She nodded. "I'm a little hesitant to put the course back on the schedule."

He nodded. "Afraid of another attack on your classroom?"

"Yes." Ouida Mae sighed. "But I don't want anyone else injured because of my choice of subjects to teach."

"Then again, these kids need the information in order to make better choices."

"True. I'll feel better when they catch the guy who trashed my classroom." She looked him over. "You didn't bring a lunch, did you?"

He shook his head. "I was focused on my first day of teaching."

Ouida Mae opened her lunch bag, pulled out a sandwich wrapped in a zip-lock baggie and handed it to him. "I hope you like ham and cheese."

He pushed it back toward her. "I can't take your lunch. It wouldn't hurt me to miss a meal, anyway."

She snorted. "Like you have an ounce of fat anywhere on your body. Take it. I made two in case you forgot to bring something."

"Always taking care of others," he said, opening the bag and taking a bite.

"That's our Miz Mo," the woman on her right said.

Ouida Mae turned to the woman. "Valentin, you remember Ms. Durrand from our day of painting?"

He swallowed quickly. "I do. It's good to see a familiar face."

Ouida Mae introduced him to the other two teachers seated around the table—all females. Valentin felt like he stuck out like a sore thumb among them. But they were all friendly and eager to give him all the feedback they'd heard from the students who'd been in his morning PE classes. The students due to attend those classes in the afternoon were eager to find out what all the hubbub was about.

"So, Harley Quinn, huh?" Ms. Durrand cocked an eyebrow. "I'd pay money to see you dressed as Harley Quinn."

All the ladies in the teacher's lounge shouted, "Me, too!"

Ouida Mae laughed. "Why Harley Quinn?"

Valentin shrugged. "Because she's female, which would make the kids want me to dress like a girl—the more embarrassing, the better. And because she's a badass." In a whisper, he added, "Like you and Sophie."

Ouida Mae's cheeks flushed a pretty pink.

Holy hell, he wanted to kiss her. There in the teacher's lounge, in front of God and everybody.

"What do you have planned for the Gifted and Talented class?"

"I want to find out what they're working on. If they're between projects, I think I'll have them do something geared toward community service. A team project to design, create blueprints, determine supplies needed and build a tiny home for a homeless veteran."

"Wow," Ms. Durrand said. "That's ambitious."

"Where will they get the money for the supplies?" another teacher asked.

"That could be one of their challenges," Valentin said. "Perhaps they could write a grant proposal or come up with a fundraiser for the project."

"Will you be here to see it through?" Ouida Mae asked. "What happens to the project when Ms. Sutton returns?"

Valentin frowned. He hadn't really thought about

another teacher taking over. "I could consult with the students and Ms. Sutton to help them to completion. The Bayou Brotherhood Protectors could provide volunteer hours for the actual building of the home. The students would have to calculate the hours and contribute their own time to construction. Not only would they be gaining experience in design, project control and hands-on construction, but they would be helping a veteran, someone who fought for their country and now needs help getting back on his feet. They could plan to have the veteran help in the construction to build his confidence, sense of worth and pride in his own home."

"I feel like I should stand and sing the National anthem at this point." Ms. Durrand said, her expression sincere, not snarky at all.

"Me, too," said the other teachers around the table.

"Us, too," said the teachers at the other tables around the room.

Ouida Mae grinned. "It's a great idea. Where do we sign up?"

Valentin's brow furrowed. "It's just an idea at this point. I want to see where the class stands with current projects before I go further."

"If the project is a go, let us know what we can do to help," Ouida Mae said.

"I think the students would get a charge out of it," one of the teachers at their table said.

"They could get the entire school involved in the fundraising and hands-on labor," Ms. Durrand said.

Ouida Mae laid a hand on Valentin's arm. "Look at you fitting right in as a teacher and role model for a bunch of Junior high students. Giving them structure, helping them learn to work as a team and coming up with new and exciting ideas. Be careful, or Principal Ashcraft will insist on keeping you."

Her hand and her words warmed Valentin's arm and heart and made him feel like he could provide value, not just be a placeholder for the absent Ms. Sutton.

He thanked her for the sandwich and went to the assigned classroom to face the Gifted and Talented students, feeling a little less of a fraud. The kids were intelligent, asked pointed questions and were actually excited about the idea of building a home. By the time the bell rang to go to their next class, they had identified tasks, assigned people and started laying out a project timeline.

The rest of the PE classes went as well as the morning ones. He had Sophie in the second to the last class of the day.

She looked sad and tired. He hated seeing her so despondent and hoped she would regain some of her confidence soon. Sophie was a good kid. She fell into formation with the other kids and worked with them as a team, even when some of them treated her as if she had cooties.

She was last to leave the gym when the bell rang.

Valentin pulled her aside for a moment. "I'm proud of how you jumped right in with the others. You showed a lot of courage."

She shrugged. "I didn't want to be the one person who caused everyone to do pushups."

"Hang in there; the day is almost over."

"There's another one right behind it," she said.

"Every day will get easier."

She laughed. "Easy for you to say. You're not pregnant. Your body won't be changing over the next nine months, growing a baby that depends solely on you for gestational survival and ultimate delivery."

He blinked at her intelligent and informed response. "You're right. My apologies. You've been researching pregnancy?"

She nodded. "I used my study hall to use the computer in the library. The more I know about what to expect, the better decisions I can make. It's too bad I didn't know more before I made the decision that landed me here." Her lips twisted. "I can't change the past, but I can help shape my future."

Valentin smiled at the girl who was growing up fast. "You're smart and determined. I have no doubt you'll accomplish whatever you set your mind on."

She left the gym to hurry to her last class of the day with Miz Mo.

Valentin was glad Ouida Mae had Sophie for the last class of the day. He worried that someone or something would set off the girl, and she would run away. She needed to know she was safe with Miz Mo.

It was Valentin's job to make sure the two women were safe. The attacker was still out there and potentially could strike again since the school board had reinstated Ouida Mae's sex education course.

After witnessing Katherine Edouard's tirade against teaching sex ed in school, he wouldn't put it past her to hire someone to sabotage Ouida Mae's classroom.

But, then again, she was a politician's spouse, the president of the PTA, a Sunday school teacher and supposedly a pillar of the community. Would she hire someone to destroy school property and injure an employee of that school?

It didn't make sense. Destroying school property wasn't helping students—unless the person she'd hired had gone overboard.

The Edouard woman had used the incident to argue her point.

As far as Valentin was concerned, the woman was still in the running as a suspect and bore watching.

Who else would trash a school classroom?

Perhaps a self-righteous zealot trying to prove a point? One who might not have a child at the school and had no qualms about destroying public property.

His thoughts went to the hothead, Regis Fontenot, who'd almost picked a fight at the Crawdad Hole Saturday night.

Valentin still wondered where the man had been at the time the school was attacked. Though, what motivation would he have had for trashing the school? The man probably didn't give a damn what was taught in the schools. The only motivation he might have to do such a thing would be if he got something out of it.

The intruder hadn't taken anything of value. If Regis had been the one to cause all that damage, someone would have had to pay him.

Again, Valentin's thoughts returned to Katherine Edouard.

As students streamed into the gym for the last class of the day, Valentin had to shelf his thoughts for the moment and focus on corralling kids.

At the end of the day, he changed into his first-impression clothes. When he emerged from the locker room, he found Ouida Mae and Sophie in the hallway.

"Will we see you tonight for dinner?" Ouida Mae asked.

Valentin looked at Sophie.

The girl nodded. "We'd like it if you'd come. I'm making spaghetti."

"I love spaghetti. Thank you."

They walked out of the school together, and Valentin followed them to Ouida Mae's cottage on the edge of the bayou.

They worked together to make spaghetti and ate

together at the dinner table like the perfect little family.

Valentin could have told himself he'd accepted the invitation to better keep an eye on Ouida Mae and Sophie, but that would only have been half the truth.

He loved their company and couldn't think of anywhere else he'd rather be.

He pushed to the back of his mind that this was an assignment that would one day come to an end. He didn't realize just how soon that would be.

CHAPTER 12

OUIDA MAE HAD NEVER LOVED TEACHING MORE since Valentin had come to work at the Junior high.

Or was it that she loved having him there all day, every day? They ate lunch together and left the school at the same time with Sophie.

Every time she asked if he'd like to join her and Sophie for dinner, he'd gladly accepted. Twice that week, he'd ordered takeout and brought dinner to them. Thursday evening, he'd brought fried chicken, mashed potatoes and gravy.

Ouida Mae and Sophie had made a salad to go with it, and they'd sat around the dinner table talking about their day at school.

Mr. Jones was out of the hospital, recovering at home and not in a hurry to return to work.

Sophie had weathered four days back at school. Her classmates had stopped pointing and whispering behind her back. She studied hard and did all of her homework, improving her grades since she wasn't going hungry or sleeping alone in a shack in the bayou. She even laughed at some of Valentin's stories about how he'd been teaching his students some self-defense skills.

Nigel had put those skills to use that day when the class bully cornered him in the hallway and tried to shove him into a locker.

The skinny little nerd managed to twist the bully's arm up behind his back and made him beg to be released. Nigel wouldn't let go until the bully promised never to pick on any of their classmates again.

The bully promised. Nigel let go. Immediately, the bully went after Nigel. Herschel came up behind the bully and used the same technique, once again making the guy beg for mercy. Other members of their PE class gathered around as Herschel released the bully.

"Apparently, their solidarity scared the bully and his buddies," Valentin said. "They haven't bothered anyone since."

"Score one for the geeks and nerds," Sophie said as she rose from the table and gathered their empty plates. As she walked into the kitchen, she asked, "Are we expecting company?"

"No," Ouida Mae answered. "Why do you ask?"

"There are headlights coming down the drive."

Ouida Mae and Valentin rose from the table and walked to the front of the house as a late model pickup rumbled into the yard. When it came to a stop, the passenger door opened, lighting up the interior where a man sat behind the wheel and a woman dropped to the ground. The woman's knees buckled, but she managed to pull herself upright by holding onto the door.

Once she was somewhat steady on her feet, she staggered a few feet forward and yelled, "Sophie Saulnier! You get yer lazy ass out here right now." Her words were slurred, and she swayed so much that she had to take another step forward to keep from falling.

"Oh no," Sophie said from behind Valentin and Ouida Mae. "Why is *she* here?"

"You know that woman?" Ouida Mae asked.

"Unfortunately, yes. That's Billie Jean Saulnier," Sophie said, her tone flat, emotionless. "My mother. The driver is her latest boyfriend, Leland Smolka, the reason why I left home seven weeks ago."

"Let me see what she wants," Valentin said.

Ouida Mae stayed with Sophie in the hallway with the light off.

Valentin flipped the switch on the front porch light and stepped outside. "Ma'am, can I help you?"

The woman raised a hand to shade her eyes. "I come to collect Sophie, my thankless daughter."

"What makes you think she's here?" Valentin asked.

"My Leland heard she's knocked up and shackin' up with that uppity science teacher. 'Bout time she gets her ass home where she belongs." Billie Jean pointed at the cottage. "I know yer in there, Sophie, girl. Time to come home."

"Ma'am, when was the last time you saw your daughter?" Valentin demanded, his tone low and dangerous.

"Why, I saw her jusss the other day. Before she got sassy and run off. Two...three...days ago. Been lookin' fer her ever since."

Before Ouida Mae could stop her, Sophie charged through the front door. "You're lying!" she shouted at her mother. "I left over seven weeks ago. You haven't once looked for me. You don't give a damn about me. Never have."

Sophie kept walking toward her mother, color high on her cheeks.

Valentin came to stand beside Sophie. Ouida Mae stood on her other side.

The teenager glared at her mother. "You never cared if I lived or died, and you didn't believe me when I told you that your boyfriend tried to rape me."

Leland shoved open his truck door. "Now, that's a goddamn lie!"

"Did he tell you how he got the wound on his

hand that night you went out to buy more drugs?" Sophie asked.

"He got it fishin'," Billie Jean said.

"He got it when he tried to put his hands down my pants. I stabbed him with my knife, or he would've raped me. You left me with a pedophile."

"That bitch is lyin' through her teeth." Leland dropped down from his truck.

"Get back in your truck, Leland," Valentin said.

Leland's lip curled back. "What are you going to do if I don't?"

"Try me," Valentin said, his voice low and dangerous.

"You lying little hussy," Sophie's mother lurched forward and grabbed the girl's hair. "Yer my daughter, and yer comin' home with me where you belong."

Ouida Mae grabbed Billie Jean's wrist. "Let go of her, or I'll call the sheriff."

"Go ahead," Billie Jean said, backing away, her hand still gripping Sophie's hair. "The law won't take my own flesh and blood away from me. And I'll have you up on kidnappin' charges. You have no right to keep my daughter from me."

Ouida Mae held on tight. "Let go of her."

Headlights turned down Ouida Mae's driveway. A second later, blue lights strobed as a sheriff's SUV pulled up beside Leland's pickup.

Shelby extricated herself from her SUV and called out, "Billie Jean Saulnier, release Sophie."

"She's my daughter. I got the law on my side. She's caused enough trouble." The woman refused to let go of Sophie's hair. "She's comin' home with me. Her mother. The one who brought her into this world."

"You're hurting me." Sophie's face contorted in pain. She tried to peel her mother's fingers out of her hair.

Deputy Taylor stepped up behind the woman. "Billie Jean, release the girl, or I'll have to hit you with my stun gun."

"You got no right," Billie Jean said. "This is my girl. She's my property, and I'm takin' her home where she belongs."

"Billie Jean Saulnier," Shelby stated clearly. "I'm bringing you in for assault on a minor and abandonment. You have the right to remain silent—"

Sophie quit trying to peel her mother's fingers from her hair.

"She's mine, I tell you," the strung-out woman yelled.

Shelby pressed the stun gun against Billie Jean's neck. The shock of electricity dropped the woman to the ground. Since her hand was still tangled in Sophie's hair, the girl went down with her.

The old pickup's engine roared to life. Gravel spit out from beneath the tires as Leland backed up, pulled a one-eighty and sped away.

Ouida Mae and Valentin helped the girl to her feet.

Sophie fell into Ouida Mae's arms and buried her face against her shoulder, her body shaking.

Shelby pulled Billie Jean's wrists behind her back and secured them together with handcuffs.

When the deputy tried to get the woman to her feet, Valentin stepped forward, scooped the woman's limp body off the ground and followed Shelby to her service vehicle. She held the back door open while Valentin deposited his burden on the back seat.

"Thank you," Shelby said as she shut the door. "I'll book her and see if there's any chance of placing her in a rehab facility."

Ouida Mae stood with an arm around Sophie's shoulders. "How did you know to come? Your timing couldn't have been better."

Shelby shook her head, her lips pressed into a thin line. "I was already on my way here," she said, "to give you a heads-up."

"Heads-up for what?" Ouida Mae asked, a sinking feeling settling in the pit of her belly.

Headlights appeared at the end of the driveway.

Shelby glanced over her shoulder. "For them," she said. "Child Protective Services has come to get Sophie."

Sophie's arms tightened around Ouida Mae. "Don't let them take me," she begged. "I want to stay with you. You said I could stay."

Ouida Mae looked over the girl's shoulder at her friend. "Is there any way she can stay? I've filled out the application to become a foster parent. Can't they leave her with me until it's approved? Surely, they wouldn't remove her from her school in the middle of a semester."

Shelby shook her head. "Remy's working with Senator Anderson to see if they can push the paperwork and interviews through faster, but I'm sorry. Child Protective Services has the legal right to take Sophie into custody and place her in an approved foster home. I can't stop them. In fact, as an officer of the law, I have to make sure no one interferes with their work."

A van pulled up beside Sophie's SUV. A man and a woman got out and approached them.

"Good evening, I'm Deborah Ledbetter, and this is my colleague, Troy Preston. We're with Louisiana's Child Protective Services. We're following up on an investigation into a reported case of child neglect accusing Billie Jean Saulnier of abandoning her daughter, Sophie."

"I'm Deputy Shelby Taylor. Billie Jean Saulnier is in the back of my service vehicle. She's under arrest for assaulting a minor," Shelby sighed as she met Ouida Mae's pleading gaze and continued, "her daughter, Sophie."

Sophie's arms squeezed Ouida Mae tighter. "I'm okay. Please, I want to stay with Miz Mo."

Ms. Ledbetter frowned. "Is Miz Mo a close relative?"

"She's closer to a relative than that woman who called herself my mother," Sophie spat out as she straightened and turned to face Ms. Ledbetter.

"I'm sorry, Sophie, but we can't leave you with someone who isn't a relative or an approved foster parent," Ms. Ledbetter said, her voice gentle, her brow creased in concern. "You'll have to come with us. We're required to place you in a safe home approved by the state."

Sophie lifted her chin. "I've been taking care of myself most of my life. I don't need strangers telling me where I'll be safe. I'm safe here with Miz Mo. You can go back to your office and leave me alone."

"We'd be neglectful in our duties if we don't take you with us now," Ms. Ledbetter said.

While the woman spoke, the man closed the distance between himself and Sophie and wrapped his arms around her.

Ouida Mae cried out, "Please, don't hurt her."

"Miz Mo! Don't let them take me," Sophie cried. "Please, don't let them take me."

"I can't stop them," Ouida Mae said, tears streaming down her face.

Sophie turned to Valentin. "Mr. Vachon, please."

Valentin shook his head. "Sophie, Deputy Taylor would have to arrest us. We have to work through the system and make it all legal."

Tears ran down Sophie's face as Troy carried her squirming body toward the van. "I should've stayed in the bayou," she called out. "I never should've trusted either one of you."

Valentin pulled Ouida Mae into his arms and held her as the van drove away with Sophie.

Once it disappeared out of sight, Ouida Mae pressed her face into Valentin's chest and sobbed. "I failed her."

"I'm so sorry, Ouida Mae," Shelby said. "My hands are tied. Remy's working on it. He's got his boss, Hank Patterson, pulling whatever strings he has to speed up the approval process. If you want Sophie back, you can't skirt the system. If you do, you'll never be allowed to foster her or any other child."

Ouida Mae knew the truth of Shelby's words, but the look on Sophie's face and the words she'd thrown their way had completely broken her heart.

"We'll get her back," Valentin said. "With a US senator and Hank Patterson on it, we'll get her back."

"I have to get back to work," Deputy Taylor said. "I'll keep you informed of Remy's progress and where Sophie is placed. Sometimes, I really hate my job."

For a brief moment, Shelby rested a hand on Ouida Mae's back. Then she climbed into her vehicle and drove away.

Valentin held Ouida Mae for a long time, standing in the yellow glow cast by the porch lights.

"Come on," Valentin said. "Let's get you inside before the mosquitos find us." He turned Ouida Mae in his arms and guided her into the house.

She moved one foot in front of the other, not thinking, her mind numb with pain.

Valentin walked with her into her bedroom, sat her on the bed and bent to remove her shoes. "Sweetheart," he said as he lifted her legs onto the bed and eased her head onto the pillow, "Sophie is a fighter. She's going to be okay until we can bring her home."

Ouida Mae stared up into Valentin's eyes. "I just stood there. I didn't stop them. I failed her."

"You didn't fail her." Valentin brushed a strand of her hair from her damp cheek. "You heard Shelby. If you'd tried to stop them, you would've ruined any chance of ever getting her back."

He pressed a kiss to her forehead. "Try to sleep. Do you want me to call Principal Ashcraft and tell her you won't be at school tomorrow?"

She shook her head. "It's too hard to get a sub this late. I failed Sophie. I can't fail all my students."

"Then sleep." Valentin brushed his lips across hers. "I'll pick you up in the morning and take you to the school."

Ouida Mae clutched his arm. "Don't."

"Don't pick you up?"

"No," she whispered and pulled at his arm. "Please," she said, just like Sophie had.

"What do you want?" He leaned over to hear her whispered words.

"Stay with me," Ouida Mae said. "Hold me like you'll never let me go."

For a moment, he stared down into her eyes. Then he kicked off his shoes and lay on the bed beside her. Both still fully clothed, he pulled her into his arms and held her.

Ouida Mae lay nestled in the warmth of his embrace, absorbing his strength. As the shock of losing Sophie waned, something swelled in its place.

A need to be held, to feel alive, to press her skin against his.

She lay perfectly still, fighting the need until she couldn't a moment longer.

"Valentin?" she whispered.

"Yes?" he said, his arm pulling her closer.

"I need you," she said so quietly she doubted he could hear.

"I'm here, babe," he said.

"You don't understand," she said, her voice a little stronger. "I'll understand if you don't feel the same, but I need to feel warm all over, inside and out. To feel alive."

"Okay, how can I help you with that?" he asked.

She rolled onto her side and stared up into his eyes. "I need you to make love with me."

He lay unmoving for so long that Ouida Mae lost her nerve. "It's okay. Obviously, you don't feel the same level of desire. Never mind."

When she started to turn away, he took her hand and guided it to his groin, where his cock made an impressive tent in his tracksuit.

"I've had a hard-on every time I've left your cottage this week. But I don't want to make love just to cheer you up. When we make love, I want it to mean more."

She ran her fingers over the tip of his cock, her breathing getting more ragged by the minute. "I've gone to bed every night with B.O.B. But it's a poor second choice to what I've wanted since that first kiss."

Valentin frowned. "Who's Bob?"

She rolled away, dug in her nightstand, brought out B.O.B. and laid it across Valentin's chest. "I don't want B.O.B. anymore. I want you."

CHAPTER 13

VALENTIN LIFTED HIS HEAD, stared at the shiny metal, battery-operated adult toy and laughed. His laughter died as raging, hot desire flamed through him. He took the toy in his hand, rose on his elbow and pressed the cold metal shaft to the pulse visibly hammering at the base of her throat.

"I never would've pictured my perfect little science teacher, beloved by all her students, owning her very own—" he frowned. "What did you call it?"

Her cheeks flushed a deep pink. "B.O.B. You know, battery-operated boyfriend. "

Again, Valentin laughed. His desire for her doubled in its intensity. "Who would've guessed the junior high science teacher had a naughty side? And shiny metal versus rubber?"

"The metal was pretty and kind of space-age." Her

brow dipped. "It was the logical thing to do. I teach sex education classes. Do you know how many STDs there are out there and how easy they are to catch?" She shook her head. "I wasn't willing to risk casual sex just because I was horny. I've spent the last few years completely responsible for my own orgasms."

He slid the device lower, posing it between her breasts. "If you're completely responsible for your own orgasms, why do you want to retire B.O.B. now?"

She met his case without blinking. "I've met an amazing man that makes B.O.B. much less interesting. It takes me longer to get there unless I pretend B.O.B is you."

"Just having carnal thoughts about me gets you off?"

Without flinching, she nodded.

"Are you not concerned about those STDs anymore?" He circled the shaft around one of her breasts, imagining her naked, not fully clothed.

"Being with you makes me want to throw caution to the winds." She gave him a crooked smile. "Do you know how difficult that is for someone who likes to be in control of her thoughts, her emotions and her body? Every cell in my body is on fire with desire. For you."

Valentin traced the toy from her breast downward to the juncture of her thighs encased in tailored slacks. "For the record, and you can set your mind at ease, I'm clean."

"As am I," she whispered. "And I'm on birth control to regulate my cycle."

He increased the pressure of the smooth metal shaft, pressing it against her sex. "Then what are we waiting for?"

"Someone to make the first move." A tentative smile curled the corners of her lips.

"I believe you've already done that," he said.

Valentin rose from the bed and drew Ouida Mae to her feet. Working slowly, he removed one article of clothing at a time from her body, starting with her blouse.

She worked the zipper on the jacket of his track-suit, running it all the way down until it fell open, and then shoved it off his shoulders.

What started as a slow and deliberate peeling of their outer clothing soon turned into a frenzied free-for-all where they took matters into their own hands and stripped the remaining clothing from their own bodies.

Once they stood totally naked in front of each other, Valentin gathered Ouida Mae in his arms, tipped her chin up and claimed her mouth in a long, heart-pounding kiss.

When he finally came up for air, he bent, scooped her up his arms and laid her gently on the bed.

"How do you feel about foreplay?" he asked.

Her chin tilted up, and she cocked a sassy eyebrow. "I want it all."

"Perfect," he said as he lowered himself over her without crushing her. "Because I want to explore every inch of your body, starting here." He touched his lips to the soft skin beneath her ear lobe.

She leaned her head back, giving him more space to work with as his mouth as he moved down the length of her throat, pausing to flick his tongue against her wildly beating pulse.

He didn't stop there for long, skimming across the swell of her breasts to capture one dusky rosebud between his teeth. As he gently nibbled and swept his tongue over the nipple, it contracted into a tight little button. While rolling it with his tongue, he cupped her other breast with his hand and squeezed gently. Then he moved to treat the other nipple to the same tender teasing.

Ouida Mae moaned, and her back arched. Her fingers slipped into his hair as she urged him to continue. With a subtle shift in pressure, she guided him downward.

Eager to comply, he brushed his lips across her ribs, moving ever lower. His hand, inches ahead of his mouth, curled over her sex. With a single finger, he found her damp entrance and slipped inside.

Ouida Mae lifted her knees and dug her heels into the mattress, raising her hips. "Please," she moaned.

Valentin moved down her body and settled between her legs.

Her knees fell to the sides, giving him full access to plunder her pussy.

With his thumbs, he parted her folds and blew a stream of warm air over her clit, quickly following with a flick of his tongue.

"Holy moly," she exclaimed.

He did it again and again until he had her writhing beneath him.

"So. Much. Better. Than... B.O.B.!" she cried.

He chuckled against her sex and sucked her clit into his mouth, alternating between gently pulling and sweeping his tongue over the tightly-packed bundle of nerves. All the while, he slipped his fingers into her wet channel and pumped them in and out.

Her body tensed beneath him.

One... two... three more flicks with his tongue, and she cried out, "Yes!" Her body froze for a moment, and then she rocked with the force of her release.

Valentin didn't let up on his campaign until Ouida Mae collapsed against the mattress, breathing hard, her body radiating heat as if she'd just run a half marathon.

With his dick rock-hard and aching, Valentin rose over her and leaned close to whisper in her ear, "What's it to be? Missionary? Doggy? Sixty-nine?"

"What part of I want it all, did you not understand?" she said, her voice low, gravelly and sexy as hell. "Start with sixty-nine. I want to taste you."

"Do you prefer bottom or top?" he asked as he brushed a kiss across her lips.

"Top," she said. "If I can move. I feel like my muscles and bones had a total meltdown."

"Take your time." He kissed her eyelids patiently when he wanted to take her hard and fast.

"No time. I don't want to waste the aftershocks of that incredible orgasm." She planted her hands against his shoulders and pushed him over onto his back. She moved over him, positioning her knees on either side of his head and her mouth over his straining cock.

As she lowered herself over him, she took his shaft into her warm, moist mouth.

He gripped her ass, drew her down over his mouth and drove his tongue into her channel, swirling, teasing and tasting her essence.

Ouida Mae sank lower, taking in his cock all the way to the base when it bumped against the back of her throat.

As she raised her head, she swept her tongue along the shaft until she reached the head. For a long moment, she circled it, flicking nibbling, then she went down again, sucking him in, the fingers of one hand curling around his balls.

Once again, he found her clit and teased it as she began moving up and down, increasing the pace of each pass until he took over and pumped his hips, fucking her mouth.

When the pressure built to the edge of his control, he lifted her off him and moved her to his side, still on her hands and knees. In a swift motion, he rolled and came up on his knees behind her. Gripping her hips firmly, he drove into her slick, tight channel, sinking deeply until his balls pressed against her.

He paused to allow her to adjust to his girth and to give him a moment to regain control. He wanted this to last as long as possible for her pleasure as well as his.

"Don't stop," she said and lowered herself to her elbows, her rounded ass high and gorgeous. When he eased out, she rocked back against him. "Faster," she urged, her voice strangled as if she couldn't quite catch her breath.

Valentin increased the pace, moving faster and faster, thrusting deep. This time, when he reached the peak, he didn't hold back. He slammed home, burying himself as deeply as he could go. Then he bent over and reached around to stroke her clit as his cock throbbed his release inside her.

He held her like that until the last waves of his release ebbed. Valentin slid free of her, eased her down to the mattress and spooned her naked body against his.

Ouida Mae chuckled softly and pressed her back closer to his front.

"What's so funny?" he asked.

Ouida Mae held up the sex toy. "With foreplay like that," she said, "I can retire B.O.B."

He took the shiny metal shaft from her hand. "I don't think you should. How do you feel about a threesome?" He skimmed the toy over her breasts and downward to the juncture of her thighs.

She eased her legs open enough he could slip B.O.B. between them. Then she guided it to her highly lubricated channel, letting him press it into her.

At the same time, his rock-hard cock slipped between her butt cheeks.

"Yes or no," he whispered against her ear.

"Yes!" she exclaimed. Reaching one hand down to B.O.B., she switched it on. B.O.B. immediately started vibrating, enough so that Valentin's cock could feel it and was stimulated back to full-on, ready-to-fuck status. Still damp from being inside Ouida Mae, his dick easily slid between her cheeks. With B.O.B.'s assistance, Valentin and Ouida Mae soared to another amazing orgasm, collapsing against each other, spent and completely satiated.

As they drifted off, Valentin whispered, "We'll get our little family back together. I promise."

How he would manage that, he wasn't sure, but he couldn't give up on Sophie or Ouida Mae. They'd become so much a part of him he couldn't lose them.

He was so passionate about it that he'd even consider the dreaded "C" word.

Commitment.

Strangely, he didn't dread it or want to avoid it.

He wanted to embrace it like he'd embraced Ouida Mae.

CHAPTER 14

OUIDA MAE'S alarm woke her the next morning at the normal time on a normal school day in her normal town.

But nothing was normal and hadn't been since a week ago when her classroom had been destroyed, and she'd met Valentin, took in a pregnant teen, lost her and made love to a man she'd known only a week.

Her normal, safe life had been turned upside down. In the process of pulling herself together, she'd learned that normal was safe, but she'd been missing out on so much.

Ouida Mae stretched, opened her eyes and glanced over at the ma—

Empty pillow beside her.

She sat up straight in bed, still naked, her pleasantly sore sex a reminder of the incredible night she'd shared with Valentin.

Speaking of which... Where had he gone? "Valentin?" she called out.

No response. A glance at her clock made her squeak. Normally, she showered at night. Given the circumstances and then making love with the PE teacher, she had missed that portion of her normal routine.

"Fuck normal," she said out loud, flung back the sheets, swung her legs over the side and stood. For a moment, she swayed. "I'm out of shape," she murmured and then wondered how one got in shape for physically demanding sex.

By having it more often.

She grabbed clean underwear and a bra and raced to the bathroom across the hall. After a quick shower, she slipped into her thong underwear and her lacey bra and dragged a brush through her tangles. After a brief attempt at scrunching her curls, she ran out of the bathroom into a solid wall.

Of male muscles.

Valentin caught and held her. "Umm," he said. "I liked you in this outfit once before. Still do, but I like you even better in nothing at all."

She melted against him at his sexy declaration. Ouida Mae wrapped her arms around his waist and pressed her cheek against his chest. "You were gone when I woke up. I thought maybe you ran off full of regret."

He chuckled, lifted her chin and smiled down at her. "No regrets," he said. "I got up earlier, ran back to my room at the morning house, showered, changed into clean clothes and got back here in time to take you to work, as promised." He grinned down at her. "Is this what you plan to wear to work? If so, none of your students are going to get anything done, not with their sexy, near-naked teacher standing at the head of the class."

His hand slipped lower and cupped her butt cheeks. "I've been wanting to do that since I saw you the first time wearing nothing more than what you have on now."

"Do you want to go back to bed and make love again?" she asked.

"I sure do."

"Too bad." She stepped out of his arms and marched toward her bedroom. "Should have gotten back fifteen minutes earlier," she called over her shoulder. "We barely have 15 minutes to get dressed and get to the school before the bell rings."

He swept her up in his arms and deposited her on the bed. "It doesn't take fifteen minutes if you do it right." His hand slipped beneath the elastic band of her thong and between her folds to stroke her clit.

He brought her from zero to near orgasm in four well-placed strokes.

"We don't...have time," she gasped. "I'm not even dressed."

He stripped her thong down her legs and tossed it aside. "Four minutes. That's all I ask."

"Only four?"

Valentin went down on her, using his tongue to bring her to sensory overload and mind-blowing orgasm in one and a half minutes.

Still pulsing from her own release, she shoved the waistband of his track suite down, freeing his long, hard cock. Ouida Mae guided him to her entrance, gripped his buttocks and slammed him home. She set the pace hard and fast, her body building up again to her second orgasm for the morning.

For a second, she teetered on the precipice.

When Valentin gave a final thrust, going as deep as he could, he remained buried for a full minute while Ouida Mae rocketed into her own bonus orgasm. When she returned to earth, she stared at the clock.

"Four minutes," Valentin rose from the bed, brought her to her feet and patted her naked bottom, his hand lingering there. "You have five minutes to dress. I made sandwiches before I left for the boarding house. Hustle!"

Ouida Mae and Valentin entered the bathroom together, each taking a clean cloth, soaking it under the sink faucet and wringing it out.

Ouida Mae used hers to clean their lovemaking from his hard cock, while Valentin used his to cup her sex and wipe away all evidence of their coupling with a final stroke of his finger across her sensitized clit.

He gave her a brief, hard kiss, then turned her toward her bedroom with a reminder, "Three minutes."

After grabbing another pair of panties from her drawer, Ouida Mae stepped into them, dragged a pair of dark trousers up her thighs, buttoned and zipped, then passed on the button-up shirt she'd planned to wear, opting for a quick pullover. She slipped into her shoes and ran for the door where Valentin waited.

They hurried into his truck, stretched some speed limits and arrived at the school with three minutes to spare.

As they walked toward the school, Ouida Mae sighed. "I almost feel guilty for making love with you last night. With Sophie, God knows where, I shouldn't be selfishly enjoying sex."

"Having regrets?" Valentin asked.

She shook her head and smiled. "No regrets over the sex. The timing, maybe, but never the sex. I'm worried about Sophie."

"I checked with Remy this morning on my way back to your place. He's meeting with Senator Anderson at the Department of Children and Family

Services today to see what they can do to speed up your approval."

"I hope they can make it happen really soon. That sweet girl needs some good things to happen for her."

"Agreed." He stopped short of entering the school and turned toward her. "I'm staying after school to work with my students on more self-defense lessons. We'll only be an hour if you can wait that long for me to take you home."

She smiled. "I can wait. I need to work on some more lesson plans and figure out when I'm going to reschedule that sex education course."

"I'd kiss you, but there are too many curious eyes already watching us," Valentin said.

"I'll take a rain check," she said.

They walked into the school like any other teachers and parted ways, going to their separate classrooms.

Worrying about Sophie made the morning drag by for Ouida Mae. She couldn't wait for lunch to find out if Valentin had heard anything from Remy.

He hadn't heard anything. No call, no text.

She ate the sandwich he made for her. Several of the teachers stopped by with their condolences over Child Protective Services taking Sophie away from Ouida Mae.

Their concern and empathy only made Ouida Mae feel worse.

If she'd thought the morning was slow, the afternoon moved at glacial speed. When the last bell rang, Ouida Mae had the start of a headache pressing at her temples. She glanced at the clock and sighed. It was Friday. She didn't want to work on her lesson plan, but she had an hour to wait for Valentin to finish his self-defense lessons with the students.

She packed her things in a satchel and debated staying in her classroom or joining the students in the gymnasium. Her third choice was to go to the bathroom first and then decide.

Ouida Mae left her satchel on her desk and hurried to the teachers' lounge and the bathroom only teachers and administration were allowed to use.

As she made her way back to her classroom, it struck her. It was Friday a week ago, at around the same time, that her classroom had been breached and trashed. So much had happened since then. The fact that it had happened exactly one week ago gave her an uneasy feeling.

A loud crash, much like the one she'd heard that fateful day, made her jump. Her startlement quickly morphed into anger, pushing Ouida Mae's logic to the back of her consciousness. She marched down the hall and turned into her classroom, ready to kick ass and take names.

A man dressed in black with a black ski mask covering his face had just climbed through the same window that he'd broken the week before.

His back was to her when he straightened and turned to grab one of the student desks to fling it into other desks.

Ouida Mae bubbled up. "What the hell do you think you're doing? I will not stand by and let you trash my classroom again. If you've got a beef with me, bring it."

The man spun to face her.

About that time, Ouida Mae's logical brain kicked in. The man was well over six feet tall. Ouida Mae barely stood at five feet tall. He could easily overwhelm her as he had Mr. Jones.

As quickly as her anger had surged, it slipped away, leaving her exposed and in fight or flight mode. A quick glance around for a weapon brought her to the conclusion that her best choice was flight.

As she spun to leave the room, the man in the black mask pushed through the desks, heading straight for her.

Ouida Mae burst out of the room and into the hallway, her shoes sliding across the smooth tiles. That loss of traction cost her.

She'd only taken three long strides when the man in black caught her by her hair and yanked her to a stop.

Ouida Mae drew in a deep breath and screamed at the top of her lungs, praying the admin staff in the office hadn't already left for the weekend.

No one came out of the office as the man pulled

her backward, slamming her body into his. He wrapped his arm around her neck and squeezed hard, cutting off the air she needed to scream.

Ouida Mae kicked and twisted in a desperate attempt to free herself. He'd trapped one of her arms under his. With her free hand, she tried to pry the man's arm away from her throat before she passed out or died.

No amount of effort on her part made him loosen that arm. She wished she'd accepted Valentin's offer to join his class that afternoon.

Then, she remembered watching a video about self-defense. She reached up and behind herself with her free hand, hoping to gouge the man in his eye. After hitting his nose and then his cheek, her thumb finally made contact with his eye.

The man cursed. His arm loosened. Ouida Mae let her body go limp, dropping out of his hold. Once she hit the floor, she rolled away and leaped to her feet.

"Goddamn bitch, you'll pay for that," the man yelled and chased after her.

Ouida Mae's only hope was to make it to the gymnasium where Valentin was conducting his self-defense training. Unfortunately, the gym was on the opposite end of the school from her classroom. She'd never been a fast runner, but if she wanted to live, she had to stay ahead of the man in black.

As she ran, she screamed like a banshee, over and

over, praying someone in the gymnasium would hear her cries.

This time, she made it to the office before the assailant caught up with her again and flung himself at her, tackling her to the ground.

Ouida Mae hit the ground hard enough that the air rushed out of her lungs. Before she could scramble to her feet again, the man threw himself on top of her, pinning her to the ground. He pulled her hair, lifting her head off the floor. "You stupid bitch. Between you and the brat, you've caused enough trouble.

"Let go of me," Ouida Mae said. "The sheriff is on his way."

"The hell he is. They're working a vehicle fire on the highway north of town. They won't be coming this way anytime soon. It's just me and you."

"And me," another voice said from the other end of the hallway close to the gym. "Let her go, and I might consider letting you live."

"Come closer, and all I have to do is twist just to break this bitch's neck." As if to demonstrate his point, he pulled back harder on her hair.

Ouida Mae cried out.

Valentin's lips formed a tight line, and his jaw hardened. "Let her go. You don't want to add murder to your rap sheet. If you let her go, I'll let you leave. No one knows who you are. They won't catch you."

"No way. I'm taking her with me as insurance." He

lurched to his feet, yanking Ouida Mae up by her hair.

Before he could get her in another headlock, Ouida Mae twisted and slammed her palm upward, hitting the man in his nose.

He screamed, released her hair and pressed his hands to his face. Ouida Mae darted away from him, heading straight for Valentin.

When the man in the black ski mask realized he'd lost his ticket out of there, he turned and ran out the front door of the school, right into a cluster of the students Valentin had just released from their after-school lesson.

Valentin and Ouida Mae ran after the man. As soon as they cleared the door, Ouida Mae yelled to the students, "Get back!"

Too late.

The assailant grabbed Nigel by the wrist and yanked the boy toward him. "Come any closer, and I'll hurt the kid."

Valentin and Ouida Mae stopped in their tracks.

Nigel exchanged a glance with Valentin.

Out of the corner of her eye, Ouida Mae saw Valentin give an almost imperceptible nod to the boy.

The skinny little nerd twisted, ducked beneath the man's arm, grabbed his wrist and shoved it up between his shoulder blades.

With the man being over a foot taller and three

times Nigel's weight, it wouldn't be long before he overpowered the kid.

Valentin and Ouida Mae rushed forward, but not before half a dozen of the lingering students reached Nigel and the assailant first. Big Boy Herschel hit the man in the side, knocking him to the ground. One of the other boys jumped on his back and picked up where Nigel left off, shoving the man's arm up between his shoulder blades.

The man rocked back and forth in an attempt to unseat Herschel and almost succeeded.

All the boys and girls came to Herschel's rescue and dog-piled on the man in black. He wasn't going anywhere.

One of the students who hadn't found a piece of the attacker to sit on stood. "I'll be right back." He ran back into the school.

"Do you guys want me to take over?" Valentin asked.

They replied as one, "No, sir!"

"We can hold him until the sheriff gets here," Hershel said.

Valentin pulled his phone from his pocket, called 911 and reported the incident. "Dispatch will have Deputy Taylor call us back. In the meantime, we need to secure this guy."

The kid who'd run back into the school reappeared, carrying several long zip ties. He handed them to Valentin. "They use these in all the cop shows. I saw them in the janitor's storage closet one day when I was hiding from some of the bullies."

Valentin took the zip ties from the kid and secured the attacker's ankles first. "Okay," he said. "One at a time."

As the boys rolled off the man in the ski mask, Valentin bent over and grabbed the man's free hand, relieved Herschel of the hand he had pushed up between the guy's shoulder blades and quickly bound his wrists together.

"You can get up now, Herschel. By the way, that was a great tackle. Have you considered trying out for the football team?"

Herschel shrugged and then shook his head. "No, their heads get hit too many times. It scrambles their brains. Plus, my mom always told me the geeks will inherit the earth. I'm good with being a geek now that I know how to take care of the bullies."

Valentin turned to Nigel and gave him a high five. "Dude, get a little meat on your bones, and you'll make a great Navy SEAL."

Nigel's eyes shone. "You really think so?"

Valentin nodded. "Absolutely." To the rest of the students, he said, "Though Nigel and Herschel got him down, you all kept him down. You couldn't do that without excellent teamwork. I'm proud of you."

He grabbed the man on the ground by the shoulder and jerked him up into a sitting position. "And who do we owe our excitement to today? Miz

Mo, since this man has caused you the most grief, do you want to do the honors?"

Ouida Mae stepped closer to the man on the ground. She reached out and plucked the ski mask off his head. "Regis Fontenot. Aren't you on probation? Your shenanigans will add more lines to your rap sheet and more years behind bars. You better hope Mr. Jones lives, or you can add murder to your list." She threw the ski mask back at him. "What is it that comedian says? Can't fix stupid."

Valentin stared at the man. "What made you trash a classroom? You can't possibly give a damn about whether or not Miz Mo teaches sex ed. Did someone pay you to trash her room?"

Regis gave them a stubborn, stony face.

"You might be able to get a plea bargain if you tell us who hired you. Was it Katherine Edouard?"

"Ha!" Regis laughed. "That woman is so busy trying to run the community she has no idea what her husband's up to. She just keeps spending money like it grows on trees. She's never stopped to ask her husband where he got it."

Ouida Mae tilted her head as if considering the man. "But you're smarter than her. You know where he got the money to fund his campaign, don't you?"

Regis snorted. "Just because she has a law degree doesn't make her smarter."

"That's right," Ouida Mae said. "Booksmart isn't the same as street smart, is it?"

"That's right," Regis said. "Even her husband, with his fancy degrees, didn't read the fine print when the leader of a certain cartel offered to fund his campaign. Now, they're calling the shots, and he has to go along with it, or they'll leak information to the press. Not only would his campaign be over, but he'd also be spending time in the jail cell next to me."

"What shots are the cartel calling?" Valentin asked. "I can't believe they're concerned about sex education being taught in the junior high."

"They don't give a rats ass about what's being taught in the school," Regis said.

"Then why did Mr. Edouard hire you to trash my classroom?" Ouida Mae asked.

"Can't say," Regis said.

"How did you know the sheriff's department would be busy handling a vehicle fire north of town?" Valentin's eyes narrowed. "Because you set the fire."

"To keep them busy while you came back to trash my room again," Ouida Mae crossed her arms over her chest. "It was a distraction."

"Ding. Ding. Ding," Regis smirked. "Give the science lady a prize."

Valentin picked up from there. "Since the cartel is pulling Mr. Edouard's strings, they forced him to come up with something to distract the local law enforcement from the real crime taking place. That helps clear the path for them to move through this area undetected."

Ouida Mae's brow twisted. "Trashing my class-room was a distraction?"

"With his wife making a big stink about sex ed in the classroom, it was easy enough to piggyback on her community activism." Regis smirked. "It was my idea. Mr. Edouard just wanted me to deflect atten-tion from the bayou whenever the cartel has ship-ments come through. Their supplier drops them off at an abandoned shack. The cartel picks it up and distributes it to their sellers on the streets of New Orleans, Atlanta and Houston. No one thinks to look in a pissant town like Bayou Mambaloa."

A sheriff's vehicle pulled into the parking lot. Deputy Shelby Taylor eased out from behind the wheel and hurried toward them. She shook her head when she saw Regis sitting on the ground, his ankles and wrists zip-tied. "Regis Fontenot. Figures. You never could stay out of trouble," she said. "I hope you like prison food because you're going to be spending a lot of time there." She turned to Valentin and Ouida Mae. "Was anyone hurt?"

"No," Valentin said.

"I was," Regis protested. "The science teacher assaulted me. I could sue."

"Shut up, Regis," Shelby said over her shoulder. To Valentin and Ouida Mae, she added, "I have backup on the way to collect this loser. Thanks for detaining him."

"Thank these students." Valentin waved a hand

toward the geeks and nerds. "They detained him. All I did was secure him with zip ties."

Shelby cocked an eyebrow at the students. "I'm impressed. Thank you for doing my job for me."

Valentin filled the deputy in on what Regis had revealed.

Shelby got on her radio to dispatch. "Contact the DEA. Apparently, we have a cartel moving drugs through the bayou."

After she hooked her mic back on her web gear, the pregnant deputy pressed a hand to her back and faced Ouida Mae. "I got some bad news as I was on my way here."

Ouida Mae pressed a hand to her chest. "Sophie?"

Shelby nodded.

"Where did they place her?" Ouida Mae demanded. "With some horrible family who won't love and protect her like I would?"

"I'm afraid not," Shelby said. "They didn't even make it to New Orleans before she slipped through their hands. Apparently, they stopped at a gas station. Sophie said she needed to use the restroom. When she'd been in there quite some time, they had the station clerk unlock the door only to find that Sophie had slipped out a small window and disappeared."

"It happened last night, and this is the first time you've heard that she's missing?" Ouida Mae clapped the hand over her mouth. "Oh my God. Sophie's out there alone and pregnant."

"Any idea where she would go?" Shelby asked.

Ouida Mae shook her head. "Before I took her in, she spent six weeks living in an abandoned shack in the bayou. No electricity, no water and relying on her boyfriend to bring her food. She only left the abandoned shack when a boat showed up and dropped one of its passengers at the shack and left. With someone else living in her shack, she had nowhere else to go."

Regis laughed. "Wouldn't it be funny if it's the same shack the cartel is using to stage the product?"

Ouida Mae's eyes widened, and her heart sank into the pit of her belly. She turned to Valentin. "Sophie has nowhere else to go. She might try to go back to that shack and see if the man is gone. If he and his friends find her…" She touched Valentin's arm. "We have to find her."

"She never told us where that shack was located," Valentin reminded her.

"Didn't she say her boyfriend brought her food? He would know how to get there." Ouida Mae started for Valentin's truck. "We have to get to Chase. Now."

Shelby called out, "Ouida Mae, I'll call for assistance. Let law enforcement handle this. The cartel is dangerous."

"Chase might be the only one who knows how to find Sophie," Ouida Mae said. "We have to get to him. He could be in danger as well if he goes out there looking for her."

Valentin caught up with Ouida Mae, unlocked the truck door and handed her up into the passenger seat. He ran around to the other side, slipped into the driver's seat and pulled out of the parking lot. "Do you know where Chase lives?"

"In the big house in the middle of town."

"The one that throws all the fancy parties?"

"That's the one."

Less than two minutes later, Valentin parked in front of the Edouards' house. Ouida Mae was out of the truck and halfway up the front steps before he caught up with her.

She punched the doorbell and paced as she waited for someone to answer.

Katherine Edouard pulled open the door. "You! Why are you here? Did you come to gloat? I can't believe the board sided with you. Our children aren't ready—"

"Shut up, Katherine," Ouida Mae said.

"How dare you come to my house and tell me to shut up?" She started to slam the door.

Valentin stuck his foot in the door to stop her. "We need to find Chase. It truly is a matter of life and death."

"It's always drama with you, isn't it, Miz Mo?"

Ouida Mae said again, "Katherine, please, for the love of God, shut up and listen."

The woman stared at Ouida Mae, shocked that she'd dared to speak that way to her.

Valentin said, "Sophie is missing, and Chase might be the only person who would know where to find her. She's in grave danger. We need to get to her ASAP."

"He stopped seeing that tramp months ago. Why would my son know where to find her now?" Katherine demanded.

"Because I didn't stop seeing her," a voice said behind Kathrine.

She turned to face her son as he descended the staircase behind her. "But you told me you quit seeing her."

"I lied," Chase said. "You could never see past Sophie's mother. But I could. She has a big heart, she's smart and she wants to live a better life than her mother. I love Sophie. I kept seeing her all this time."

"But she's pregnant," Katherine said.

Chase nodded. "With my child."

CHAPTER 15

KATHERINE'S FACE BLANCHED. "No. That can't be right. You're too young."

"We thought the same," Chase said. "We didn't think we could get pregnant. I was in shock when Sophie texted me last Saturday from Miz Mo's phone."

"She used my phone to text you?" Ouida Mae asked.

"Yes, she was upset about a piglet. You had taken her out to Bellamy Farms," the young man's lips twisted. "She wasn't making sense. When she said she was pregnant, I thought she was kidding. She wasn't."

"Chase, have you seen Sophie?" Valentin asked.

Chase frowned, shaking his head. "She hasn't talked to me since the school board meeting. I heard Child Protective Services picked her up last night. I thought they had her."

"She got away from them," Ouida Mae said. "She has nothing but the clothes on her back. Do you have any idea where she would go?"

"Wasn't her mother hauled off to jail?" His brow furrowed.

"Could she have gone to her mother's house since her mother isn't there?" Valentin asked.

"No way," Chase said. "Her mother was hauled off to jail. If that bastard, Leland, wasn't hauled off as well, he's probably living in her mother's house. There's no way Sophie would go back there. You know he tried to rape her, right?"

"Yes, she told us," Ouida Mae said. "She mentioned a shack in the bayou where she lived for the last six weeks. Could she have gone back there?"

"I don't know how far down the road they got before she escaped, but that shack is the only place I know she might go back to. If she can get there, that's where she'll go."

"Chase," Valentin said, "could you show us where that shack is in the bayou?"

"Did she say anything about the men in the boat?" Chase asked. "Did she know if they finally left?"

"We don't know," Ouida Mae said. "We're worried she might've gone to the shack, and those men could still be there."

"Do you know who the men are?" Katherine asked.

"We think they're with a drug cartel," Valentin said.

"Actually, your husband might know more about those men than we do," Ouida Mae said.

Katherine's perfectly sculpted brows twisted. "How would my husband know?"

"You'll have to ask him the details," Valentin said. "Apparently, they loaned him the money to continue his campaign. With the cartel money, strings are always attached."

"My husband would never take money from a drug cartel," Katherine said.

"And teenagers can't get pregnant," Ouida Mae said softly. "All I know is there's a young girl out there who's alone and afraid. I don't want her to fall in the hands of that cartel."

Chase pushed past his mother and out onto the porch. "I'll show you where the shack is."

Kathryn reached out and grabbed her son's shoulder. "It's too dangerous. You can't go out there."

"If it's too dangerous for me, it's dangerous for Sophie," Chase said with remarkable maturity for a fifteen-year-old. "I have to help them find her."

"I forbid it," Katherine cried.

"You can't stop me, just like you couldn't stop me from seeing Sophie." He hugged his mother. "I have to do this."

Chase climbed into the backseat of Valentin's truck. Ouida Mae and Valentin got in the front.

Valentin shifted into drive and pulled out onto Main Street. "I assume you have access to a boat?" he asked, glancing at the boy in the rearview mirror.

"My father keeps a fishing boat down at the marina. I know where he hides the key," Chase said. "That's how I got out to the shack to take food to Sophie."

Valentin drove to Marceau's Marina, parked his truck in the parking lot, took his Glock out from beneath his seat and tucked it into his waistband.

"Wow," Ouida Mae said. "I hope we don't have to use that."

"Me, too," Valentin said.

Chase led the way to a slip along the dock where a fancy fishing boat was moored. He dropped into the boat and fished out a key from under the driver's seat.

Valentin handed Ouida Mae down into the boat, then got in beside her.

Chase expertly drove the boat out of the slip and into the bayou. He maneuvered around bends and tributaries until he slowed to a stop and moved to the front of the boat to engage a smaller and quieter trolling motor.

They moved forward slowly through a tunnel of overhanging trees.

Valentin sent a text to Remy, pinpointing their location and asking him to share that information with the sheriff and to send backup.

Remy replied, wanting him to wait for that backup.

They couldn't, not if Sophie was in grave danger. Every minute counted.

Chase stopped the boat in the shadow of a willow tree. "The shack is just around the bend, on a small island, tucked into the trees."

"You two stay here," Valentin said. "I'll check it out."

"How are you going to do that without the boat?" Ouida Mae whispered.

"The water is only waist deep, maybe a little more."

When he swung his legs over the side of the boat, Ouida Mae grabbed his arm. "You can't just wade through the bayou. It's full of snakes and alligators."

"It's a short distance," Valentin assured her. "I won't be in the water long." He brushed a kiss across her lips. He turned to Chase. "If I'm not back in ten minutes, take Miz Mo back to the marina and send the sheriff after me. He'll have my pin location and won't need you to lead him here." He held Chase's gaze. "Will you do that?"

Chase nodded. "Yes, sir."

Valentin slipped as quietly as possible into the murky bayou, holding his Glock above the water. His gaze scanned for the tell-tale sign of alligators lurking nearby like floating logs with eyes.

As he neared the little island, voices drifted through the trees—male, angry voices.

As Valentin reached the island, he crawled up the bank and moved silently through the underbrush toward the voices.

"How could you let the bitch get away? If she gets back to town, she'll bring the law back before we make the transfer," a man said. "Find her. This time, silence her for good. She can't be far, this island isn't that big. We sank her boat. She'd be insane to swim away in this alligator-infested swamp. Go!"

Valentin lay low as a man tromped through the brush inches away.

Once the man had passed, Valentin moved closer until the shack came into view. He'd approached from a side angle and could see the front porch that served as a dock. The shack had been built on stilts a few above ground. An airboat was tied to a piling. He counted three men—one on the dock and the other two on the boat with several ice chests stacked neatly on the deck, marked in bold letters, FISH.

"They should be here by now," a heavyset guy with tattoos on his arms and neck said.

"They'll be here," said another guy who wore khaki slacks, a navy-blue polo shirt and sunglasses. He also wore a shoulder holster with what appeared to be a .45- or .9-millimeter handgun tucked inside.

The man on the dock leaned against a post, his tattooed arms crossed over his chest, his beard long and shaggy. He had a knife seated in a sheath clipped to his belt on one side and a handgun in a holster on the other side of his belt.

A movement caught his eye in the limited crawl space beneath the shack. His first thought was *alligator.*

As he studied the figure, he realized it wasn't an animal. It was a mud-covered girl.

Sophie.

To get to her, he'd have to go through four men.

He could tell the moment Sophie spotted him. She raised a finger to her lips and pointed to the water beneath the dock. Valentin had no idea what she wanted him to do.

The girl slid through mud until she reached the water and submerged.

She surfaced at the rear of the airboat with a line in her hand and tied it to the steel cage surrounding the giant fans used to propel the boat. Then she sank into the water, disappearing beneath the surface. If he hadn't seen her, he wouldn't have been able to tell what was a fish or a girl moving along the murky bottom of the bayou toward him.

Valentin edged backward toward the water in the shadows of the trees, his gaze trained on the water's surface, searching for alligators. If the men on the boat or the dock spotted Sophie, Valentin was prepared to shoot.

He concentrated on his breathing and focused on

everything around him. Somewhere on that island was a man sent to kill the girl.

Not on Valentin's watch.

Sophie surfaced nearby like a water nymph, her nose clearing the water just enough to breathe.

Valentin slid into the water with her and pointed in the direction of the fishing boat.

Staying in the shadows and as submerged as possible without getting his weapon wet, Valentin pointed and urged Sophia forward in front of him, prepared to turn and provide cover for her.

They'd reached the bend in the tributary when a shot rang out. A bullet ripped through the leaves of an overhanging willow.

"She's getting away! And there's a man with her," a voice shouted.

Valentin shoved Sophie around the bend and spun to return fire.

Once Sophie was out of range, Valentin rounded the corner and moved as fast as he could half-wading, half-swimming through the bayou.

When the boat came into his view, Sophie was almost halfway there.

Chase stood in the bow of the boat, pointing frantically at the water. "Gator!" he called out.

"Come on, Sophie," Ouida Mae cried. "Swim faster."

Sophie gave up all effort to move quietly through

the water and swam as fast as she could toward the boat.

The gator was closing on her fast.

Valentin aimed his weapon and fired at the gator before it got too close to Sophie.

He either hit it or scared it because it slowed to a stop.

Sophie kept moving, now only ten yards from the boat.

Ouida Mae and Chase leaned over the side. As soon as Sophie came within range, they grabbed her hands and dragged her over the edge of the boat.

Valentin was still twenty yards out.

The gator had disappeared.

The roar of an airboat's fan filled the air.

Valentin didn't have time to worry about an alligator. There were four armed men on an airboat who would be within range all too soon.

He moved as fast as he could through the water, the floor of the bayou sucking at his shoes. As Valentin neared the boat, Ouida Mae appeared with an oar in her hands.

Sophie and Chase leaned over the side of the boat as Valentin reached them. When he started to pull himself up over the edge, Ouida Mae swung the oar so close to him he felt the whiff of air against his face.

When the oar connected with something in the water, Ouida Mae raised it and swung again.

Valentin's legs still dangled in the water. He had

just swung one up over the side when a sharp pain ripped through his calf, and he was dragged downward toward the water.

"The gator's got him," Ouida Mae cried. Using the oar like a club, she slammed it over and over again into the alligator's head.

The reptile's teeth ripped through Valentin's pants, and the animal dropped back into the water.

Valentin scrambled aboard the bass boat. "Use the big engine," he told Chase. "Get us out of here as fast as you can."

The teenager revved the 450-horsepower engines on the back of the boat, spun it around and shoved the throttle forward. The boat sped through the bayou, Chase steering it easily around tight corners.

But a bass boat wasn't an airboat. It couldn't go across marshes without the propellers getting bogged down in the shallows.

All Valentin could hope was that the line Sophie had tied to the back of the steel cage slowed the airboat from taking off long enough for them to put considerable distance between them.

Valentin prayed Remy had received his message and had their backup on the way.

They came to a point where the only way to get back to the marina was to cross a wide-open area of tributaries, weaving through a marsh.

There was no avoiding it.

As soon as they emerged from the shadows of the

overhanging trees into the open, Valentin looked back to find the airboat gaining quickly on them.

When they got within range, Valentin could fire on them, and they could return fire.

"Sophie, Ouida Mae," Valentin called out over the roar of the engines, "get in the bottom of the boat and keep your heads down. Chase, you, too."

"No, sir," Chase said, refusing to give up the helm. "You don't know the bayou like I do. If we make the wrong turn, we could bog down in the shallow marsh."

Valentin couldn't argue with that, but he didn't want the kid to take a bullet.

Soon, they didn't have a choice.

The airboat was in range of his pistol. Valentin open fire, doing his best to make each round count. But with the boat bouncing on the water's surface, it was hard to aim and even harder to hit the target.

Three of the four men returned fire while the fourth drove the airboat. They were gaining quickly and would overtake them soon.

Valentin continued to fire until he ran out of ammunition.

With the airboat almost on them, he pushed Chase out of the way and shouted for him to drop to the bottom of the boat. Valentin ducked as low as he could and still see over the bow. Bullets struck the boat and shattered the windshield in front of him.

Valentin couldn't give up. Three souls on board were depending on him.

Pain stung his shoulder. He knew he'd been hit, but he still had full use of the shoulder. Just a flesh wound, like the gator bite. He didn't let it slow him down.

He was going so fast that he missed the turn in a tributary and plowed into a marsh. Immediately, the propellers sank into the shallow mud. The boat bogged down, coming to a complete stop.

Valentin abandoned the helm and flung himself over Ouida Mae and Sophie, praying he could shield them and stop the bullets from entering their bodies.

He waited for the men on the airboat to come abreast, bracing himself for the bullets that would surely tear through him and into the women below. He tensed, ready to leap to his feet and throw himself at the murderous cartel members.

The roar of the airboat fans changed and began to move away from the bass boat stuck in the marsh.

Another engine roared nearby.

Valentin raised his head in time to see an airboat with a sheriff's decal on it race past them in pursuit of the cartel's craft. Another airboat trailed behind the first. This one had a DEA emblem prominently displayed.

The airboats were quickly followed by one of the bass boats the marina rented to tourists. This last boat came to a stop close to the Edouard's grounded bass boat.

Remy waved at Valentin and called out, "Is everyone all right?"

Valentin rolled away from Ouida Mae and Sophie. "Are you ladies okay?"

"I'm fine," Sophie said.

"Me, too," Ouida Mae reported.

"Chase?" Valentin glanced over to where the teenager still lay at the bottom of the boat. His gut clenched.

"Chase?" Sophie cried and scrambled across the boat toward the boy.

Finally, the kid groaned. "I'm okay," he said, "but I might need some help getting up. I think I broke my arm."

Sophie knelt on the floor of the boat beside him, gripped his shoulders and rolled him over into her arms. "Oh, Chase, you'll do anything for attention." She winked and pressed a kiss to his cheek.

Remy threw a line to Valentin. He tied it to the front of the bass boat and let Remy's boat pull them as he adjusted the tilt of the bass boat's big motors. With a little finagling, they freed the boat, and Valentin was able to follow Remy back to the marina.

Katherine Edouard, her mascara smeared and her hair in disarray, stood on the dock. When she spotted her son, tears welled, and she rushed forward.

Sophie helped Chase to his feet. Remy and Valentin assisted him as he climbed out of the boat.

Cradling his arm against his chest, Chase turned away from his mother and waited for Sophie to step onto the dock. "Sophie, we need to talk."

She smiled gently. "After you have your arm looked at."

He shook his head. "No. I don't want to risk losing you again. I want to marry you and raise our baby together."

Sophie cupped his cheeks in her hands. "I want what's best for our baby. Being raised by teenagers too young to drive sets us up for failure, and our baby will struggle along with us. We're too young to raise a child on our own. We need to finish high school and go to college or a trade school."

"I want to be a part of our baby's life," Chase said. "It's part of you and me. I love you, Sophie."

Chase's mother stepped forward.

Ouida Mae intercepted her and whispered, "They were old enough to make a baby; they're old enough to discuss options."

Valentin loved that Ouida Mae wanted the young people to make their own...informed decisions.

"I don't want to end up unemployable because I couldn't afford the time or cost of getting a degree," Sophie said. "I don't want that for you, either. I'd like to speak with a counselor and get all the information before we make a decision."

"Together," they said simultaneously.

She smiled and brushed her thumb across his lip. "You will always be my first love, Chase Edouard."

"I love you, Sophie, and always will," he said.

"Now, let your mother take you to get that arm looked at. If I'm gone when you get out of the hospital, don't worry, I will be back..." she said, "when I can return legally. I'm done running away. It's time I faced my problems and my future with courage."

Valentin's heart swelled with pride for a girl who wasn't his daughter, but he'd be proud to call her daughter any day of the week.

Ouida Mae slipped an arm around his waist and leaned into him. "I love that girl. I'm going to do everything in my power to be a part of her life."

"If her mother releases her for adoption, I'd snap her up in a heartbeat." Valentin chuckled. "And to think, I never thought I wanted children."

"I always have," Ouida Mae admitted. "But I'd hoped to start with a baby of my own." She sighed. "Endometriosis might keep me from realizing that dream. I accept that, but I have so much love in my heart I would adopt or foster a great kid like Sophie in a heartbeat."

Deputy Shelby Taylor walked toward them, clutching a hand to her swollen belly. "The ambulance is here. Anyone willing to share one with a woman in labor?" She doubled over, her face creased in pain. "Yup, that was a strong one. I just want to write up my report before I..." Again, she doubled over. "Screw the report. I'm taking that ambulance. Will someone notify my husband that I'm on my way to deliver his child? If he wants to remain married to me, he'd better get his—" Shelby doubled over, grunting like an animal.

Ouida Mae hurried over to her friend. "Shelby, get into the ambulance. I'm not qualified to deliver a baby. Besides, I need to get Valentin to the hospital for an alligator bite and gunshot wound. So, be a good girl and get in the ambulance."

"I'm going," Shelby said. With the help of a paramedic, the deputy climbed up into the back of the ambulance. The door closed, and Shelby was whisked away.

Another ambulance pulled into the marina parking lot. "Chase, Valentin, you're up," she called out.

"Ever consider a career as a drill instructor," Valentin murmured as he passed her and let the paramedic help him into the back of the ambulance. He sat on a bench inside and held out his good arm to help Chase in and settle beside him.

The medical technicians got busy stabilizing the two patients and stowing their gear.

"Katherine and I will meet you two at the hospital in Baton Rouge," Ouida Mae called out as they hurried to Katherine's car.

Since they'd resolved the mystery of who had

sabotaged Ouida Mae's classroom and hurt Mr. Jones, and Mr. Edouard had been taken in for questioning for his involvement in drug trafficking through the bayou, Valentin's services were no longer needed to protect Ouida Mae and the school.

The assignment was over. He had no reason to continue working there or to spend time with the pretty science teacher. He could go back to his work as a Brotherhood Protector, and Ms. Sutton could resume her position as the PE and Gifted and Talented teacher.

Or could he finish the semester with the students and then transition back to being a protector...?

A blur of movement caught Valentin's attention as Remy raced up from the dock.

"Remy," Valentin called out. "We need to talk."

Remy blew past him, shouting, "Later, dude. My baby is having a wife!"

EPILOGUE

"SOPHIE, HURRY," Ouida Mae called out. "We're going to be late." She gathered the baby in her arms and held her warm little body, her heart filling with so much love she felt she might explode.

At a month old, Harley Quinn had captured their hearts with her sweet face and happy cooing.

Valentin emerged from their bedroom, dressed in the suit and tie he'd worn on their wedding day, his beard neatly trimmed and his thick hair slicked back.

He still made her stomach flutter and her knees weak. She suspected he would, even when they were old and gray.

"Valentin, could you grab the diaper bag?" Ouida Mae asked. "I have the baby. We're headed out to the truck."

Sophie emerged from her bedroom in the beautiful pink and white floral sundress she'd chosen on their last shopping trip to New Orleans. Ouida Mae's hairdresser had given the girl the perfect cut that made her rich dark curls frame her lovely face.

But it was the sparkle in her eyes that made her shine so brightly.

Ouida Mae balanced Harley on one arm and pulled Sophie close with the other. She was so blessed and filled to the brim with love; it welled in her eyes and slipped down her cheeks in happy tears.

"Today's the big day," she said as she straightened and brushed the moisture from her face.

Valentin handed her a tissue from the box he carried. He knew her better than she knew herself.

Ouida Mae leaned up on her toes and kissed her wonderful, thoughtful husband who'd never wanted to teach kids but had learned to love it during his short stint working at the Bayou Mambaloa Junior High.

"You said you wouldn't cry," Sophie said. "Now, you're making me cry." The teenager wiped the tears from her own eyes.

Ouida Mae had sworn, over and over, that she would not cry. It made her eyes red and her face blotchy.

Felina was bringing her camera to the courthouse in Thibodaux to record the event. Ouida Mae wanted to frame the pictures and make copies for Sophie and

Harley, commemorating the day they were adopted and became part of the Vachon family.

As a family, they'd return to Bayou Mambaloa to be a part of the community celebration to hand over the keys to the house the middle school students had designed and built with the help of the teachers, the town and the Brotherhood Protectors.

Jimmy Sorenson, the homeless veteran chosen to receive the house, had been involved in the building process and the color, tile, carpet and furnishing choices. He'd contributed hours of sweat equity into his home, regaining confidence and self-respect along the way.

The local construction contractor who'd consulted on the project had been impressed with Jimmy's dedication, work ethic and ability to catch on quickly. Halfway through the project, he'd hired Jimmy full-time as a construction laborer and had taken him under his wing to teach him the art of finish carpentry and cabinet making. He saw the potential in Jimmy to eventually take over his construction business.

While the home was being built, Jimmy had been moved from living on the streets of New Orleans to Bayou Mambaloa. Remy had insisted on the veteran living in the boarding house until the project was complete.

Surrounded by other former military men, Jimmy

had made new friends and fit right into the cama-
raderie of brothers in arms.

Valentin plucked Harley Quinn from Ouida Mae's
arms, gave her a loud kiss on the cheek and carried
her out the front door of the cottage. "Are your
parents following us to the courthouse," he asked as
he settled the baby into her car seat and tightened the
straps.

"Are you kidding?" Ouida Mae laughed. "They left
fifteen minutes ago. We're going to be late if we don't
get a move on."

Valentine dropped another kiss on Harley's cheek
making the baby smile. He straightened and smiled
across the back seat at Sophie. "Are you still sure
about all of this?"

Sophie nodded. "Positive. We both want what's
best for Harley. You and Miz Mo will give her the
best life." A smile spread across her face, and more
tears welled in her eyes. "And the best part is, I still
get to be a part of her life as her sister. And if
anything ever happened to you two, you know I
would take good care of her."

"And Chase?" Ouida Mae asked as she climbed
into the front passenger seat. "Is he still all right with
the adoption?"

"He is," Sophie said. "Since his father was
convicted of drug trafficking, and his mother
divorced him and set up her own law practice in

Bayou Mambaloa, he will always have a connection to the town where his baby lives. And Miss Katherine will always be involved as a grandparent."

"Did I tell you that Katherine will be joining us for girls' poker night next Saturday?"

Sophie laughed. "That's great. I'm glad Chase's mother has come around and become more human. She seems a lot happier making her own money and decisions."

The ceremony at the Lafourche Parish courthouse was small, attended by Ouida Mae's parents, who were between trips to the wilds of different continents and happy to celebrate their daughter's new family. They loved Sophie and baby Harley.

Katherine Edouard, now Katherine Robeline since she'd changed back to her maiden name and the name displayed on her law degree, was there with Chase as he signed the documents to release custody of his daughter.

When the adoption ceremony concluded, they all hugged each other. Ouida Mae felt like these people were all part of her extended family. Her heart was full.

"Now," she said, "let's get this family back to Bayou Mambaloa for the key ceremony and the party afterward."

They piled in their vehicles and headed back home.

The whole town turned out for the ceremony to hand over the keys to the house the middle school had built for Jimmy.

The Gifted and Talented class had voted to let Nigel be the representative who would hand the keys over to Jimmy. In the past nine months, Nigel had grown in confidence and six inches in height. He'd been working out with Valentin, building muscle and stamina. He'd even joined the track team in long-distance running. Ever since Valentin had told him he had the potential to become a Navy SEAL, the boy had been on a mission to make that happen.

Ouida Mae truly believed he would realize that dream in the near future.

Hershel had also been working out with Valentin and slimmed down. He and Lori Andrews, a fellow Gifted and Talented classmate, had been seen holding hands and eating ice cream together at Sweet Temptations. They'd discovered a common interest in architecture when they'd worked together on the CAD program to design the veteran's home.

A military color guard had been sent to present the flag while Lissa Monahan sang the National Anthem.

When Nigel handed the key to Jimmy, the entire town erupted in cheers that Ouida Mae was sure could be heard all the way to New Orleans.

A band played zydeco music from the gazebo, food trucks and tented booths ringed the park as people spread out blankets on the grass and settled in to eat great Cajun food and visit with their friends and neighbors.

Sophie and Chase wandered off to join classmates playing volleyball at one end of the park. After giving birth to Harley, Sophie had gone back to school with purpose and determination. No longer weighed down by teen pregnancy and her mother's legacy, she was blossoming into a confident young woman while at the same time recapturing the joy of youth.

She wanted to finish high school with a high GPA, go to college and become either a psychologist or an attorney who could help children like her who hadn't won the lottery in parents and suffered abuse and neglect.

Chase wanted to be an engineer, join ROTC and enter the military as an officer. He and Sophie were still seeing each other but were super cautious when it came to intimacy.

After going through pregnancy and delivering a healthy baby girl, Sophie preferred to abstain from further forays into sex until she was ready to start a family. She vowed to wait until after she'd gotten her degrees and was able to support a child.

The Bayou Brotherhood Protectors and their families took up a big portion of the grass they'd covered in blankets and quilts.

Shelby and Remy spent most of their time corralling Jean-Luc, their ten-month-old baby boy.

Though he hadn't committed to walking, the baby crawled faster than a mouse tempted by cheese, keeping his parents on their toes.

Geneviève, Gerard and Bernie's baby, born two months before Sophie gave birth, lay next to Harley Quinn beneath the pop-up sunshade they'd erected to keep the little ones cool in the hot Louisiana sun.

Ouida Mae looked around at her friends and family and smiled.

Valentin nuzzled her neck. "What are you thinking about?"

"I'm looking at how much good came from a series of bad decisions. None of our happiness would've happened if Harvey Edouard hadn't made the decision to accept money from the cartel for his campaign. When the cartel put the squeeze on him to create a distraction, he made his next poor decision by hiring Regis Fontenot."

Valentin picked up from there. "Katherine Edouard's poor decision to launch a campaign to shut down your attempt to educate middle school students on the consequences of unprotected sex had a couple of repercussions."

Ouida Mae nodded. "It gave Regis the idea, and he made his poor decision to trash my classroom, making it look like some of Katherine's doing, shifting attention to the school and away from the bayou."

"Delaying the sex education course meant Chase

and Sophie didn't have the knowledge to make the right decisions when they engaged in intimacy," Valentin said.

"Billie Jean's decision to let her boyfriend move in with her and her daughter forced Sophie to find other living arrangements." Ouida Mae's lips twisted. "Which led her to the shack in the bayou. The cartel's decision to use that shack to stage their drug transfers forced Sophie to, again, seek alternative living arrangements."

"Which led her to you," Valentin said. "That was her best decision. You are the smartest, kindest person I know. She couldn't have chosen better."

"Because Sophie made the bad decision to skip out on Child Protective Services and return to the shack, she was almost killed," Ouida Mae said.

"But wasn't," Valentin added. "Her decision to go there led us, the sheriff and DEA to the shack. That netted the arrest of four of the cartel's key drug traffickers, Harvey Edouard's arrest and confiscation of cocaine and fentanyl."

Ouida Mae leaned over to kiss her husband. "The good that came of Regis's decision to trash my classroom was you. I might never have met and fallen in love with you if you hadn't come to work as the PE and Gifted and Talented teacher. The nerds and geeks learned how to defend themselves, and the Gifted and Talented took your idea and leadership and built a house. Jimmy has a home, job and a community."

"To top it all, we're married, have two beautiful daughters and a life full of love now and in our future," Valentin said. "As a man who never wanted to commit to a relationship, I couldn't have made a better decision when I committed to all of this."

ATHENS AFFAIR

BROTHERHOOD PROTECTORS
INTERNATIONAL BOOK #1

New York Times & USA Today
Bestselling Author

ELLE JAMES

BROTHERHOOD PROTECTORS

INTERNATIONAL

ATHENS AFFAIR

New York Times & *USA Today* Bestselling Author

ELLE JAMES

CHAPTER 1

HIRING on with the Jordanian camera crew as their interpreter hadn't been all that difficult. With Jasmine Nassar's ability to speak Arabic in a Jordanian dialect and also speak American English fluently, she'd convinced the Jordanian camera crew she had the experience they needed to handle the job. However, the resume she'd created, listing all the films she'd worked on, had probably lent more weight to their decision.

Not that she'd actually worked on any movie sets. Her ability to "be" anything she needed to be, to fit into any character or role, was a talent she exploited whenever needed since she'd been "released" from the Israeli Sayeret Matkal three years earlier.

Her lip curled. Released was the term her commanding officer had used. *Forced out* of the special forces unit was closer to the truth. All because of an affair she'd had with an American while she'd been on holiday in Greece. Because of that week in Athens, her entire life had upended, throwing her into survival mode for herself and one other—her entire reason for being. The reason she was in Jordan about to steal the ancient copper scroll.

The Americans arrived on schedule for the afternoon's shoot at the Jordan Museum in Amman, Jordan. The beautiful film star Sadie McClain appeared with her entourage of makeup specialists, hairstylists, costume coordinators, and a heavy contingent of bodyguards, including her husband, former Navy SEAL Hank Patterson.

Sadie was in Jordan to film an action-adventure movie. All eyes would be on the beautiful blonde, giving Jasmine the distraction she'd need to achieve her goal.

Much like the movie heroine's role, Jasmine was there to retrieve a priceless antique. Only where Sadie was pretending to steal a third-century BC map, Jasmine was there to take the one and only copper scroll ever discovered. The piece dated back to the first century AD, and someone with more money than morals wanted it badly enough he'd engaged Jasmine to attain it for him.

Up until the point in her life when she'd been driven out of her military career, she'd played by the rules, following the ethical and moral codes demanded by her people and her place in the military. Since the day she'd been let go with a dishonorable discharge, she'd done whatever it took to survive.

She'd been a mercenary, bodyguard, private investigator and weapons instructor for civilians wanting to know how to use the guns they'd purchased illegally to protect themselves from terrorist factions like Hamas.

Somewhere along the way, she must have caught the eye of her current puppet master. He'd done his homework and discovered her Achilles heel, then taken that weakness in hand and used it to make her do whatever he wanted her to do.

And she'd do it because he had her by the balls. He held over her head the one thing that would make her do anything, even kill.

Her contact had timed her efforts with the filming of the latest Sadie McClain blockbuster. The museum was closed to the public that afternoon but was filled with actors, makeup artists, cameramen, directors and sound engineers.

The American director had insisted on an interpreter, though Jasmine could have told him it was redundant as nearly half the population of Jordan spoke English. Part of the deal they'd struck with the Jordanian government had been to employ a certain percentage of Jordanian citizens during the production of the movie. An interpreter was a minor concession to the staffing and wouldn't interfere with the rest of the film crew.

Plus, one inconsequential interpreter wouldn't be noticed or missed when she slipped out with the scroll in hand.

For the first hour, she moved around the museum with the film crew, reaffirming the exits, chokepoints and, of course, the location of her target. She'd visited the museum days before as a tourist, slowly strolling through, taking her time to examine everything about the building that she could access, inside and out.

The scroll was kept in a climate-controlled room away from the main hallways and exhibits. Since the facility was closed to the public, there wouldn't be anyone in the room.

While the crew set up for a scene with Sadie McClain, Jasmine slipped into the room to study the display cases once more.

The copper scroll had been cut into multiple pieces. Each piece had its own display case with a glass top, and each was locked. She'd brought a small file in the crossbody satchel she carried, along with a diamond-tipped glass cutter in the event the locks proved difficult. Cutting glass was the last resort. It would take too much time and could make too much noise if the glass shattered.

She'd honed her skills in picking locks and safecracking as a child, one of the many skills her mother had taught her. She'd insisted Jasmine be able to survive should anything ever happen to her parents.

Her mother had been orphaned as a small child in the streets of Athens. To survive, she'd learned to steal food and money, or valuables that could be sold for cash or traded for food.

From picking pockets and swiping food from stores and restaurants, she'd worked her way up to stealing jewelry, priceless antiques and works of art from the rich all around the Mediterranean. She'd used her beauty and ability to quickly learn new languages to her advantage, infiltrating elite societal circles to divest the rich and famous of some of their wealth.

She'd gone from a starving, barefoot child, wearing rags in the streets of Athens, to a beautiful young woman, wearing designer clothes and shoes and moving among the who's who of the elite.

Her life had been what she'd made of it until she'd met Jasmine's father, a sexy, Israeli Sayeret Matkal soldier, at an Israeli state dinner attended by wealthy politicians, businessmen and their wives. She'd just stolen a diamond bracelet from the Israeli prime minister's wife.

The special forces soldier outfitted in his formal uniform had caught her with the diamond bracelet in her pocket and made her give it back as if the woman had dropped it accidentally.

Rather than turn her in for the theft, he'd kept her

close throughout the evening, dancing with her and pretending she was just another guest.

Her mother had fallen for the handsome soldier and agreed to meet him the next day for coffee. Less than a month later, they'd married.

For love, her mother had walked away from her life as a thief to be a wife and mother. But she'd never forgotten the hard lessons she'd learned on the streets. She'd insisted her daughter learn skills that could mean the difference between independence and dying of starvation or being reliant on someone who didn't give a damn about her health or happiness.

Her mother had taught her what school hadn't, from languages, dialects and staying abreast of the news to learning skills like picking locks, safe cracking, picking pockets and hacking into databases for information. She'd learned skills most parents didn't teach their children or warned their children to avoid.

Jasmine had earned her physical capabilities from her father. As an only child, she'd been the son her father never had. As an elite Sayeret Matkal, her father had kept his body in top condition. Jasmine had worked out at home with him and matched his running pace, determined to keep up with the father she loved so fiercely.

He'd taught her how to use a variety of weapons and the art of defending herself when she had no weapons at all. Because of her dedication to conditioning, her hand-to-hand combat skills and her ability to speak multiple languages, when she'd joined the Israeli military, she'd been accepted into Sayeret Matkal training soon after.

After the Athens affair and her subsequent release from the elite forces, she'd continued her training.

Now, due to circumstances out of her immediate control, she was on the verge of stealing from a museum the priceless copper scroll the Jordanians were so proud of.

Her jaw hardened. If she had to steal every last item in the museum, she would—anything to get Eli back alive.

She pulled the file from her satchel, glanced toward the room's entrance and then bent to stick the file into the little keyed lock. She fiddled with the lock until she tripped the mechanism, and the lock clicked open.

Jasmine tested the case top by lifting it several inches and then easing it back down. One down, several more to go. She'd work them a few at a time. When she had all the locks disengaged, she'd take the scroll and walk out of the museum or leave with the Jordanian film crew.

She cringed at the thought of waiting for the crew to head home. They could be there well into the night, filming take after take until they perfected the sequences.

No, she'd head out as soon as she could. She had a deadline she would not miss—could not miss—if she wanted to see Eli again.

Jasmine jimmied the locks on a few more of the displays and then returned to where the crew was staging the next scene with Sadie McClain.

In the shadow of a statue, one of Sadie's bodyguards shifted, his eyes narrowing. He wore a baseball cap, making it difficult to see his face.

Something about the way he held himself, the line of his jaw and the dark stubble on his chin struck a chord of memory in Jasmine. A shiver of awareness washed over her. She hurried past him without making eye contact.

When she looked back, the space where he'd been standing was empty.

Jasmine shook off a feeling of déjà vu and stood near the Jordanian camera crew, interpreting when needed but basically remaining quiet and out of the way.

With the preparations for the big scene complete, the camera crews stood ready for the director to shout *action*.

All other personnel were to move out of the line of sight of the cameras. This gave Jasmine the opportunity to slip back into the room with the copper scroll. When she heard the director shout, *"Action,"* Jasmine went to work quickly and efficiently, lifting the tops off the glass cases one at a time, wrapping each piece of the copper scroll in a soft swatch of fabric she'd brought in her satchel, handling them carefully so as not to break the fragile copper.

Jasmine placed each piece inside a box she'd designed specifically for transporting the delicate scroll. Once all the pieces were stored, she closed the box and slid it into her satchel.

Taking the extra time, she returned all the tops of the glass cases to their original positions so they wouldn't draw attention until a museum employee just happened to notice the cases were empty. That should buy her time to get the items out of the museum and out of Jordan before anyone became suspicious.

With her satchel tucked against her side, Jasmine hurried out of the room. At that moment, the director yelled, "Cut!" He motioned to the film crews and gave orders to the American and Jordanian cameramen.

Some of the Jordanians looked around for their interpreter.

Ready to get the hell out of the museum, Jasmine had no choice but to approach the cameramen and provide the necessary translation for the director. All the while, her hand rested on her satchel, anxiety mounting. The longer she stayed in the museum, the greater the chance of someone discovering the copper scroll was missing.

Short of racing out of the building and drawing

attention to herself, she remained, forcing a calm expression on her face when inside she was ready to scream. A life depended on her getting out of the museum and delivering the scroll—Eli's life.

ACE HAMMERSON—HAMMER back in his Navy days— thought he recognized the interpreter as soon as she'd stepped through the museum doors with the Jordanian camera crew. The more he studied her, the more he was convinced it was her.

Jasmine.

The woman with whom he'd spent an amazing week in Athens. A week he could never forget.

Had it really been four years?

Granted, she looked different from the last time he'd seen her. She'd changed. Her dark hair peeked out from beneath the black scarf she wore over her head and draped around her shoulders. Her curves were hidden beneath a long black tunic and black trousers. Her face was a little thinner, but those full, rosy lips and her eyes gave her away. There was no mistaking the moss green irises that had captivated him from the first time he'd met her at an outdoor café in the Monastiraki district of Athens.

He'd come to Antica Café on a recommendation from a buddy who'd been there a year earlier. The place had been packed, with no empty tables left. Tired and hungry after the twenty-hour journey from San Diego to Athens, he'd just wanted to eat, find his hotel and crash.

Rather than look for a less crowded café, he'd looked for an empty seat. A beautiful woman sat in a far corner, a book in her hand, enjoying a cup of expresso. Ace had approached, hoping she wouldn't blow him off, and asked if she spoke English.

She'd looked up at him with those amazing green eyes and smiled. In that moment, he'd felt a stirring combination of lust, longing and... strangely...home-coming wash over him. It could have been exhaustion, but more than hunger made him want to join this woman at her table.

She spoke English with a charming accent he couldn't place as either Greek or Arabic. When he'd asked if he could share her table, she'd tilted her head and stared at him with slightly narrowed eyes before finally agreeing with a relaxed smile.

That had been the beginning of the most incredible week of his life. His only regret was that he'd had to go back to work after that week. Before he'd had time to look her up, based on the phone number she'd given him, he'd deployed for several months to Afghanistan, where the mission had been so secret, they'd gone incommunicado to avoid any leaks.

By the time he'd returned to his home base, her number had been disconnected.

He hadn't known where to begin looking for her. In all their conversations, she'd barely revealed much about her life other than both her parents were dead, having been killed in a Hamas strike in Israel.

Because of her reference to her parents being killed in a Hamas strike, he'd assumed she was from Israel. She'd talked about her mother having been from Greece and her father from Israel. Like him, her father had been on vacation in Athens when he'd met her.

Ace had searched for her online, hoping to find out something about her whereabouts, but failed miserably. On his next vacation, he'd gone back to Greece, to the same restaurant where they'd met, hoping by some strange coincidence he'd find her there. He'd walked the same paths they'd walked through the city, looking for her. He'd stayed in the same hotel where they'd stayed, even insisting on the same room.

She hadn't been there. He'd gone to Tel Aviv and talked with some acquaintances he'd met during joint training exercises with the Israeli military. They hadn't heard of her.

As many people as there were in Israel, Ace hadn't expected to find her just by asking around. But he'd hoped that the same magic that had brought them together the first time would help him find her again. After a year, he'd admitted defeat and tried to forget her.

That had never happened. Every woman he'd dated after Jasmine had never sparked in him the fire and desire he'd felt with the woman he'd met in Athens.

Now, here he was, freshly out of the military, working with Hank Patterson and his team of Brotherhood Protectors in Amman, Jordan. Nowhere near Athens and four years after that fated affair, she walked back into his life.

New to the Brotherhood Protectors, Ace had agreed to accompany Hank and members of his team to Jordan to provide security for the film crew and actors who were friends of Hank's wife, Sadie McClain, on her latest movie set. He'd be an extra, there to observe one of the team's assignments.

They didn't always provide security for film crews, but since significant unrest existed in the countries surrounding the relatively stable Jordan, the film producers and studio had budgeted for a staff of security specialists.

Hank had worked with the studio and cut them a deal to ensure his people provided security for his wife and the crew there to make movie magic. Brotherhood Protectors were the most qualified to provide the safety net they might need if fighting spilled over the borders from countries surrounding Jordan.

Though he'd been excited and curious about the mechanics of making a movie, Ace's attention had shifted the moment Jasmine entered the museum.

His gaze followed her as she moved among the Jordanian film crew, standing between Americans and Jordanians, interpreting instructions when needed.

As the camera crew set up, Jasmine left them to wander around the museum, looking at ancient artifacts on display. At one point, she disappeared into a side room and remained gone for several minutes.

Ace started to follow when Hank approached him. "It's amazing, isn't it?"

Ace nodded. "Yes, sir."

Hank grinned. "I never imagined the amount of people it takes to produce a film until I accompanied Sadie on set for the first time."

Though Ace would rather focus his attention on Jasmine's movements, he gave his new boss all his attention. "I never realized there was so much involved."

"Right? It takes an incredible amount of coordination to set up a gig like this, from securing a location to getting permission, in this case, from the government to film here, to transporting all the equipment. Not to mention hiring people to do all aspects, including lighting, sound, video, makeup and costumes."

Ace's gaze remained on the door through which Jasmine had disappeared. "And that's just the filming," he commented, mentally counting the seconds Jasmine was out of his sight.

Then, she emerged from the room and rejoined her camera crew.

Ace let go of the breath he'd been holding.

Hank continued the conversation Ace had lost track of. "After the filming, there's the editing, music, marketing and more." The former Navy SEAL shook his head, his lips forming a wry smile. "I have so much more respect for all those names that scroll across the screen in the movie theater when they show the credits." He chuckled. "I always wondered, and now I know, what a key grip is."

Jasmine worked with the cameramen once more, then stepped back into the shadows.

Once the cameramen were in place, the lighting guy gave a thumbs-up. The director nodded, spoke with Sadie and then stepped back.

"They're about to start filming," Hank said.

When the director raised a hand, everyone grew quiet.

The director looked around at the placement of the cameras, Sadie and the lighting, then nodded.

Ace felt as though everyone took a collective breath, waiting for it...

"Action!" the director called out.

Ace's attention was divided between Jasmine, the actors, the cameramen and the supporting staff.

The beautiful, blond actress, Sadie McClain, did not command his attention like Jasmine.

Sure, Sadie was gorgeous, dressed in khaki slacks that hugged her hips, boots up to her knees and a flowing white blouse tucked into the narrow waist-band of her trousers.

Her mane of golden hair had been styled into a natural wind-swept look with loose waves falling to her shoulders. She worked her way through the museum corridor, pretending to be a patron until she arrived at a golden statue encased in a glass box.

As Sadie studied the statue, her character assessing her chances of stealing it, Jasmine slipped out of the main museum corridor into the side room again.

What was she doing in there?

Ace wanted to follow her, but to do so, he'd have to pick his way through the camera crews and lighting people. He didn't want to get in the way while the cameras were rolling. God forbid he should trip over a cable, make a noise or cast a shadow and make them have to start all over again.

So, he stood as still as a rock, all his attention on that room, counting the seconds until Jasmine came out or the director called, "Cut!"

Finally, Jasmine emerged from the room.

At the same time, the director yelled, "Cut!"

The crossbody satchel she'd worn pushed behind her now rested against the front of her hip; her hand balanced on it. Her head turned toward the museum entrance and back to the organized chaos of camera crews shifting positions and responding to the director's suggestions. An American cameraman approached the Jordanian crew and spoke in English.

Members of the Jordanian camera crew frowned, looking lost. One of them spotted Jasmine and waved her over.

Jasmine's brow furrowed. Her gaze darted toward the museum entrance once more before she strode across the floor to join the cameramen. She listened to the American cameraman and translated what he was saying for the Jordanians, who, in turn, grinned, nodded, and went to work adjusting angles.

Jasmine stepped back into the shadows.

Ace nodded to Hank. "Excuse me. I want to check on something."

Hank's eyes narrowed as his gaze swept through the people milling about. "Anything to be concerned about?"

Was there anything to be concerned about? Ace's gut told him something was off, but he didn't see a need to alarm Hank until he had a better idea of what. "No, I just want to look at some of the displays."

"Are you a history buff?" Hank asked.

"A little. I'm always amazed at artifacts that were created centuries much earlier than our country's inception."

Hank nodded. "Yeah, some of the items in this museum date back hundreds of years before Christ."

He gave Ace a chin lift. "Explore while you can. It looks like they're getting ready for another take."

His gaze remained on Jasmine as Ace strode across the smooth stone floors to the room Jasmine had visited twice in less than an hour.

The room was climate-controlled, with soft lighting and several display cases positioned at its center. At a brief glance, nothing appeared out of place, but as Ace moved closer to the display cases, he frowned. They appeared...

Empty.

His pulse leaped as he read the information plaque beside the row of cases.

COPPER SCROLL. 1ST CENTURY AD.

He circled the cases and found that they all had keyed locks. He didn't dare lift the tops off the cases. If he did, he'd leave his fingerprints all over the glass and possibly be accused of stealing what had been inside.

His stomach knotted. Jasmine had been in here. Had she come to steal the copper scroll? Did she have it stashed in that satchel she'd carried around all afternoon?

Ace spun on his heels and left the room. His gaze went to the last place he'd seen Jasmine. She wasn't there.

His pulse slammed into hyperdrive as he scanned the vast corridor where the film crew worked.

She was nowhere to be seen.

Ace strode toward the museum's entrance. As he neared the massive doors, someone opened the door and slipped through it.

That someone was Jasmine.

What the hell was she up to? If she'd stolen the scroll, he had to get it back. If he didn't, the museum would hold Hank's team responsible for the theft, especially considering they were the security team.

The copper scroll was a national treasure. If he didn't get it back, it could cause an international incident as well as delay film production.

Ace slipped out of the museum and paused to locate the thief.

Dark hair flashed as Jasmine rounded the corner of a building across the street from the museum.

Ace had to wait for a delivery truck to pass in front of him before he could cross the road. As he waited, two large men dressed in black entered the side street, heading in the same direction as Jasmine.

Once the delivery truck passed, Ace crossed the street and broke into a jog, hurrying toward the street Jasmine had turned onto.

As Ace reached the corner of the building, he heard a woman shout, "No!"

He turned onto the street.

A block away, the two men in black had Jasmine by her arms. She fought like a wildcat, kicking, twisting, and struggling while holding onto the satchel looped over her neck and shoulder. One man ripped the scarf from her head and reached for the satchel's strap.

"Hey!" Ace yelled, racing toward the men.

Jasmine used the distraction to twist and kick the man on her right in the groin. When he doubled over, she brought her knee up, slamming it into his face.

The injured man released her arm.

Jasmine turned to the other man, but not soon enough. He backhanded her on the side of her face hard enough to send her flying.

As she fell backward, the man grabbed the satchel and yanked, pulling it over her head as she fell hard against the wall of a building.

Clutching the satchel like a football, the man ran. His partner staggered to his feet and followed.

Ace would have gone after them but was more concerned about Jasmine.

The men ran to the end of the street. A car pulled up, they dove in, and, in seconds, they were gone.

Jasmine lay against the wall, her eyes closed, a red mark on her cheek where the man had hit her.

Anger burned in Ace's gut. He wanted to go after the men and beat the shit out of them. But he couldn't leave this injured woman lying in the street.

He knelt beside her and touched her shoulder. "Jasmine."

Jasmine moaned, blinked her eyes open and stared up into his face, her brow furrowing. "Ace?

What—" She glanced around, her frown deepening. "Where am I?" She met his gaze again. "Is it really you?"

His lips turned up on the corners. "Yes, it's me. You're in Jordan." His brow dipped. "You were attacked."

She pinched the bridge of her nose. "What happened?"

"Two men attacked you," he said.

"Two men..." She shook her head slowly. "Jordan..." Then her eyes widened, and she looked around frantically. "My satchel! Where is my satchel?"

"The men who hurt you took it."

She struggled to get to her feet. "Where did they go? I have to get it back." As she stood, she swayed.

Ace slipped an arm around her narrow waist. "They're gone."

"No!" She raked a hand through her hair. "I need that satchel." Jasmine pushed away from Ace and started running back the way they'd come, then stopped and looked over her shoulder. "Which way did they go?"

He tipped his head in the direction the men had gone.

When Jasmine turned in that direction, Ace stepped in front of her and gripped her arms. "They're gone. You won't catch up to them now."

"Why didn't you stop them? They stole my satchel!" She tried to shake off his grip on her arms.

His lips pressed together, and his grip tightened. "What was in the satchel, Jasmine?"

"Something important. I have to get it back. Please, let go of me."

"Was the copper scroll in your bag?" he asked quietly so only she could hear his words.

Her gaze locked with his. For a moment, she hesitated, as if deciding whether or not to trust him. Then she nodded. "I had to take it. If I don't get it back, someone I care about will die."

ABOUT THE AUTHOR

ELLE JAMES also writing as MYLA JACKSON is a *New York Times* and *USA Today* Bestselling author of books including cowboys, intrigues and paranormal adventures that keep her readers on the edges of their seats. When she's not at her computer, she's traveling, snow skiing, boating, or riding her ATV, dreaming up new stories. Learn more about Elle James at www.ellejames.com

Website | Facebook | Twitter | GoodReads | Newsletter | BookBub | Amazon

Or visit her alter ego Myla Jackson at mylajackson.com
Website | Facebook | Twitter | Newsletter

Follow Me!
www.ellejames.com
ellejamesauthor@gmail.com

ALSO BY ELLE JAMES

Remy (#1)

Gerard (#2)

Lucas (#3)

Beau (#4)

Rafael (#5)

Valentin (#6)

Landry (#7)

Simon (#8)

Maurice (#9)

Jacques (#10)

Cajun Magic Mystery Series

Voodoo on the Bayou (#1)

Voodoo for Two (#2)

Deja Voodoo (#3)

Damned if You Voodoo (#4)

Voodoo or Die (#5)

Brotherhood Protectors Yellowstone

Saving Kyla (#1)

Saving Chelsea (#2)

Saving Amanda (#3)

Saving Liliana (#4)

Saving Breely (#5)

Saving Savvie (#6)

Saving Jenna (#7)

Saving Peyton (#8)

Saving Londyn (#9)

Brotherhood Protectors Colorado

SEAL Salvation (#1)

Rocky Mountain Rescue (#2)

Ranger Redemption (#3)

Tactical Takeover (#4)

Colorado Conspiracy (#5)

Rocky Mountain Madness (#6)

Free Fall (#7)

Colorado Cold Case (#8)

Fool's Folly (#9)

Colorado Free Rein (#10)

Rocky Mountain Venom (#11)

High Country Hero (#12)

Brotherhood Protectors

Montana SEAL (#1)

Bride Protector SEAL (#2)

Montana D-Force (#3)

Cowboy D-Force (#4)

Montana Ranger (#5)

Montana Dog Soldier (#6)

Iron Horse Legacy

Drake (#6)

Grimm (#7)

Murdock (#8)

Utah (#9)

Judge (#10)

Delta Force Strong

Ivy's Delta (Delta Force 3 Crossover)

Breaking Silence (#1)

Breaking Rules (#2)

Breaking Away (#3)

Breaking Free (#4)

Breaking Hearts (#5)

Breaking Ties (#6)

Breaking Point (#7)

Breaking Dawn (#8)

Breaking Promises (#9)

Hearts & Heroes Series

Wyatt's War (#1)

Mack's Witness (#2)

Ronin's Return (#3)

Sam's Surrender (#4)

Hellfire Series

Hellfire, Texas (#1)

Billionaire Online Dating Service

The Billionaire Husband Test (#1)

The Billionaire Cinderella Test (#2)

The Billionaire Bride Test (#3)

The Billionaire Daddy Test (#4)

The Billionaire Matchmaker Test (#5)

The Billionaire Glitch Date (#6)

The Billionaire Perfect Date (#7)

The Billionaire Replacement Date (#8)

The Billionaire Wedding Date (#9)

The Outriders

Homicide at Whiskey Gulch (#1)

Hideout at Whiskey Gulch (#2)

Held Hostage at Whiskey Gulch (#3)

Setup at Whiskey Gulch (#4)

Missing Witness at Whiskey Gulch (#5)

Cowboy Justice at Whiskey Gulch (#6)

Boys Behaving Badly Anthologies

Rogues (#1)

Blue Collar (#2)

Pirates (#3)

Stranded (#4)

First Responder (#5)

Cowboys (#6)

Made in United States
Cleveland, OH
28 January 2025

13845111R00184